To those who never stop believing,
even through the fiercest of storms.

Dragons & Ravens

A Draev Guardians Novella

E.E. Rawls

Titles by E.E. Rawls

Earthaverse:

Draev Guardians Series

Strayborn (1)

Storm & Choice (0.5)

Dragons & Ravens (1.5)

Strayblood (2)

Alteredverse:

Frost, Winter's Lonely Guardian

Portal to Eartha

Beast of the Night

Madness Solver in Wonderland

Coming Soon:

Straypath (3)

Secret Projects ;)

Find out when the next books are releasing, and get exclusive content, by following my newsletter at:

eerawls.com

GOUBELIN
BERGVOLK
Mondburg
I Diviso Sea
HIGHLANDS
KING
D
Backbone Mountain
Greater
Magica
Forest
Kingdomf
Valley
Haunt Marshes
Grin Chasm
Lesser
Magica
Forest
Cla
Aq
Noncello river
ARAH SANDS
SALMU
BARIS
HUMAN
OF
XOTIPHOS

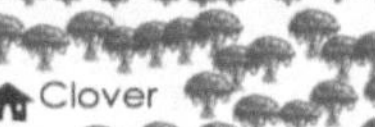

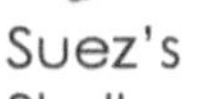

OM OF
ETH
ELDFJÖLL
SIVORTSKA
RĂSĂRIT
Lake Doroth
Morbid Dungeons
DRAETHVYLE
Outer Woods
Tantō
Mountains
Clover
ELVENSTONE
AKATSUKI
FORESTABELLA
Suez's
Skull
HIGASHI
REPUBLIC
OTIPH
EARTHA

CURSE
OF
FIRE

1

The past forms me. The past binds me. It is a curse I can never be rid of...

Eight-year-old Hercule adjusted the white cravat around his neck until his reflection in the mirror was perfection. Seated on a plush stool in his grand bedroom, he waited for Nana to enter and announce that his personal tutor had arrived and was waiting in the third private study room for him.

Lord Renald (his father) insisted that noble persons never be seen waiting for those of lower status; let the lesser people wait for them to arrive. And so, Hercule wasn't in the study, ready to begin the day's lessons, but here in his bedroom.

School. Hercule wondered what normal school would be like, a place where you interacted with other kids the same age. He had playdates with relatives and children of nobility, now and then, but it was usually when their parents were coming over for a dinner party or some fancy event at the mansion. Those aristocrat kids were... *difficult*. The boys had different ideas of the definition of "fun," and the girls weren't much better. He didn't like the girls—they were too much like his overbearing, chatterbox of a mother.

Badminton and such games that they played were lame. And his male cousins' pranks with frogs and slugs to scare the girls made him turn his nose away in disgust. Father always said a nobleman's son should never behave like a dimwit, nor do any wasteful, silly thing. He wanted to prove to Father that he was better than them.

So, he kept mostly to himself. Hercule's idea of "fun" was...was...

He frowned at himself in the mirror in thought. "*Hmph*, who cares what fun is? It won't get me anywhere in life. It has no purpose. Only dimwits waste time having fun."

"Come in," Hercule replied to a knock at the door, and Nana entered.

"Your tutor has arrived and awaits you, milord." Nana flashed a smile. The woman who had been his nanny for years cared more about his title—the sole heir of House Dragonsbane—than she did about him, and how it elevated her status to be associated with one of the great Noble Houses.

"My, I see you're looking especially handsome today," Nana pretended, bending down eye-level to view him in the mirror. Hercule's golden eyes reflected back at him. "Are you ready for your birthday celebration? I hear it's going to be quite the party!" She held her smile, waiting for his response. But when Hercule stared blankly back at her, the smile twitched.

Nana straightened back up, holding the smile tighter. She swallowed. "I can hardly believe you're turning eight years old. You seem so mature for your age! There's a rumor going round that you're to get an extra special present this year. Aren't you excited?" she tried again.

Hercule looked away as if she hadn't spoken, getting up and exiting through the paneled door. He heard Nana muttering under her breath: "Miserable child. You'd think he would be happy on his birthday—happy for at least *one* day a year."

Marching down the hallway's silk rugs on the second floor, Hercule made his way to the private study assigned for his schooling.

The morning dragged on as Hercule recited the Multiplication Table, read aloud memorized old poems of Draeth literature, aced a quiz on geography, and so on. Until at last the tall grandfather clock in the corner bonged the noon hour and signaled the end of schooling for the day—finishing early because it was his birthday.

The tutor, a tall, thin man with round spectacles on a pinched nose, gave him a bow as he departed. "Have a good birthday, milord. May there be many more to come. I shall look forward to this evening's party."

Hercule gave a small, disinterested nod.

The head butler appeared in the room briefly and said, "Your father wishes to see you in his study."

Hercule's frown tightened.

Inside Father's grand study room, Hercule stood before the great dragon-legged desk with its chiseled scales. Father looked down his nose at him. The old portraits of their ancestors to Hercule's right also seemed to be staring down at him disapprovingly.

"I trust you will behave properly at the party this evening, yes? No running, no silly games, and no dirt on your suit?

I know the other noble children can be rambunctious, but you are this House's heir, and must always be seen as perfect."

"Yes, sir."

"And mind how much you eat—I refuse to have a son who gains weight."

"Yes, sir."

"Good. Now go shower and get yourself ready."

Hercule had already showered but left to do so again.

The first half of the party began early that evening, outdoors with a spread of savory appetizers and specially crafted strawberry shortcakes. The back courtyard of Dragonsbane Mansion became all decorative tables, silver utensils and painted porcelain sets, the chairs topped with red ribbons. Servants and slaves of the House were dressed in red livery with the embroidered Dragonsbane crest on the breast: a dragon with a sword run through the heart. They meandered through the crowd of lords, ladies and aristocrat youngsters, serving tea and cannoli on glittering trays.

At least one member from each of the twelve Noble Houses was present, as was tradition for the heir of a House's birthday. But each had their own agendas, pretending to be friendly while scheming behind others' backs—the ongoing game between Houses vying for power.

'Why don't they have anything better to do?' Hercule thought while watching them, his frown twisted to one side.

He made his way through the oppressive throng of people dressed in silks and laces and embroidered cuffs—suits and cravats stiff, clean-cut; ladies' feet tiptoeing on impossibly high-heels beneath pleated dresses. There were a few extra puffy skirts and petticoats that made the wearers resemble walking bells.

A few elaborate hairstyles hurt his eyes to look at, but none could compare to the ridiculously fantastical hair of Mother: a cone-spiral, three feet high, coming to a point above her head where a red rose sprouted and let its petals fan outward; several carnations poked out around the sides of the cone to add complementary colors. It was a miracle she could walk, let alone stand, with that weight on her skull.

Hercule groaned. He could hear Mother's voice chatting away at a group, loud enough for everyone in the crowded yard to hear without trying. How she *loved* to stand out and brag! Especially for the young men's attention. Most were wise enough to keep their distance and make excuses to slip away before she could corner them like prey. But one man hadn't been so lucky: Mother was hanging on his arm, giggling and flashing flirty glances, pretending to pat his shoulder while feeling his muscles. He tried in vain to escape.

Hercule continued his way out of the crowd and away from the courtyard, toward the open field that fringed a pond. Kids of the guests were playing croquet on the lush grass, or something like it. Mostly it looked like boys bad-mouthing and teasing girls, and the girls then chasing them and waving croquet sticks threateningly. He turned his nose up and found a seat at the pond's edge. The water sparkled like diamonds in the hot summer sun. Spotted and long-finned koi swam the waters like the imprisoned decorations that they were. He could relate to those fish right now: trapped in a pond, swimming in circles with no hope of ever being free and living their own lives.

Two hours into the party, before the red-icing birthday cake was to be served, his mother, Chatsalott, brought Hercule to a long table stacked with a mountain of presents. He had no desire to unwrap this year's load, but he had no choice in the matter. The gifts that guests brought him were only for show—they could care less about what Hercule actually wanted. This was an unspoken contest for who could give the future heir of Dragonsbane the most impressive gift, each House trying to outdo the other.

Young Hercule found himself stuck in the middle of their twisted game every year, opening bags and boxes taller than himself. This year's gifts—he vaguely noted as he tore open wrapping paper—were tall porcelain pieces, exotic birds, a new portrait of himself paired with matching tapestries, a grand supply of rare *earl heavensing* tea, and other items he didn't bother keeping track of. He had to thank each guest in turn. He kept his face an expressionless mask so no one could determine which gift had pleased him more, and therefore which guest had "won" the contest. Hercule was an impartial statue, while the nobles' gazes flicked haughtily back and forth, chins raised, approving or disapproving of each gift.

By the time Hercule finished unboxing the last present, daylight was fading, and the first course of dinner was to be served. He felt exhausted but refused to let it show. Renald, his father, took the seat at the head of the indoor dining table, Mother on one side, Hercule on the other. He'd barely said a word to his son the whole party; that was the norm he was used to. So it was a surprise when he suddenly spoke.

"There is one last gift for you, from your mother and I, now that you've grown from a toddler into a boy."

Mother's face lit up and she was practically bouncing in her seat with excitement, her head of cone hair bouncing precariously with her. "Oh dearie me, yes! We've both agreed that you're old enough. I received my first when I was your age."

Hercule cocked his head, wondering what on eartha it could be.

"We'll be taking you tomorrow to choose..." Father continued, after frowning at his wife's interruption, "your own personal slave attendant."

The emerald leaves glistened warm and mysterious beneath the sunbeams penciling through the dense canopy. Young Marigold shielded her eyes as she blinked up at the golden arrows of light slanting down to the mossy forest floor, and then turned her attention back to the flowers that speckled the knobby root of an ancient oak. She picked one flower here, three blue bells there, a purple mushroom here…

She moved along, barefoot, enjoying the feel of squishy moss beneath her toes. Several adult faeryn were a distance back, chatting as they paused for a quick meal on their way back to the village in Lesser Magica Forest. She could hear Papa's voice among them. She fluttered her green luna-moth wings behind her back and tossed her thick, blonde braid.

Marigold hummed to herself, finding a periwinkle flower, placing it behind her long, pointed ear and dusting her leaf dress, when a sudden cry of alarm came from the group behind her.

She looked back over her shoulder at the noise, and that was when a thick sack came down over her head, turning the world dark.

Strong hands bound her wrists, snatched her up and threw her over a shoulder.

Marigold shouted for help, legs kicking, wings beating. But the sounds of running feet and screams from the other faeryn grew distant. The body of the shoulder she was draped over moved at a steady jog, stealing her away, and panic made her mind black out…

When Marigold regained consciousness, the world was still blinded, and she could feel metal binds digging into the flesh of her wrists and ankles. The voices of her captors rumbled around her, a coarse joke here and a laugh there.

'What's going to happen to me?' she thought and shuddered. The man carrying her had entered someplace crowded, judging by the squeak of doors and a new ruckus of voices. The sack covering her face slid down bit by bit as her torso bumped against the man's shoulder, until it finally dropped off and her eyes were able to take in the scene around her.

A grimy hall, full of vempars, came into focus: some of them armed guards, some bearing capes with a winged fang crest, all mingling and drinking as if after a hard day's work. The sour stench permeating the air curled her nose.

Ruthless gazes from a few of them watched her as she passed, and their fanged mouths smirked. She trembled, trying to shrink on the shoulder she helplessly dangled from. She couldn't even flap her wings—the man had them pinned down under his arm.

A cold draft hit her bare legs under her leaf-fabric skirt as the room was blocked from view and her captor entered a stone corridor. The solid floor dipped unevenly while he ambled down a long set of stairs. At the bottom, they passed filthy enclosures of stone and bars.

What was this vempar planning to do with her?

Behind every set of cell bars were persons. She couldn't make out much in the dim lantern light but gaunt figures either worn out or on the verge of death. Their sunken eyes stared blankly, watching as she was carried past. A few who were livelier kicked at the floor and walls as if driven mad, their skin pale and blood vessels stark from lack of sunlight.

Marigold recalled the stories older faeryn told of what happened to those caught by vempars: Some were put in a life of slavery, destined to grovel at the feet of a master who might end their life any moment on a whim. Others were locked in dungeon cells, and had their *essence* drained from them day by day to fill the vempars' food supply, until their aged bodies could be drained no more.

Fear coursed through her in tremors, making her teeth chatter together and limbs shake uncontrollably. She recalled Nonna's distant words: *"Beware the fanged ones who lurk in the shadows. If you wander too far from home, you risk becoming their prey."*

But she hadn't run off on her own! She'd been with her papa and other faeryn. She'd only wandered a few yards to pick flowers, that was all. And yet...

Her bottom lip trembled. What had happened to Papa?

An alarmed gasp tore from her throat as the vempar carrying her hoisted her off his shoulder and tossed her like a grass doll onto the cold floor of one of the dungeon cells. Landing hard on her bottom, Marigold scooted backwards on her hands and bare feet away from the man. His shadow cast by the glowing lamps on the walls swallowed her tiny form. He eyed her up and down, evaluating his day's catch like a piece of meat, lips curled in a sinister grin as if he found her fear amusing.

"I got me a fine catch!" he cackled. "Somebody'll pay a pretty coin for you, if you're lucky. And if not, your *essence*'ll make a sweet addition to our food Reservoir." He laughed at the look of terror she failed to hide, then bolted the barred door shut and left, his heavy steps echoing.

Alone now, she felt a little relief. No more fangs glistening through a twisted grin. She shivered, rubbing at her bruised arms. Every inch of her body felt bruised or scraped. She gingerly touched a painful lump on her scalp, then rubbed at her ankles where shackles continued to dig into skin, the flesh there raw and bleeding. It was the same for her wrists, but thankfully the shackles weren't as tight since her arms were unusually thin. She didn't know when the binds had become shackles; everything about the last day seemed foggy. She stretched out her wings and they slumped down, as if the dungeon itself weighed down on them.

Marigold guessed it must be night, since the air had become steadily colder. She tried to fall asleep on a small pile of hay in the corner. There wasn't much else to do; she couldn't claw her way through stone and bars and escape.

The floor and walls of the confined space felt frigid as ice on her bare legs and feet. She tried to fit all of herself on top the hay. Bangs and loose strands from her thick braid tangled about her face and shoulders. Rips and grime had ruined her once pretty leaf dress. She tried to tuck her freezing feet and shins up underneath the skirt, but it wasn't helping much to keep warm.

'I wish I'd kept my foot-coverings on...'

Something rustled. It came from the cell across from hers. She cautiously lifted her head.

The rustling continued, and curiosity got the better of her.

She crawled forward—flinching at painful bruises—to the door made of bars, and she peered out.

A hunched figure was moving about in the other cell, trying to find a better resting position, but the stones of the uneven floor jabbed uncomfortably and kept whoever it was shifting. "Do you need some more hay? I could toss you some," Marigold offered quietly. Then she repeated the words in Inglish, the common tongue, thankful for her lessons.

The person's movement halted and their head turned. Marigold could make out a human woman, very old with scraggly hair and a permanently bent back, and rags for clothes. Bony limbs creaked with her every move. "Kind offer, but no," the human said roughly. "Nothing but a feather mattress could make this old body stop aching. A pity someone young as you ended up in this wretched pit."

Marigold watched her. "How long have you been here?"

A faint cackle came from the woman. "Too long, far too long. Nobody chose me for a slave, so I've been kept here as part of the Reservoir, my *essence* taken daily. Now that I'm old, they don't have much to take. The ruthless..." she spat, "heartless, soul-sucking monsters."

Marigold flinched. Few things could be worse. "I'm so sorry," she said, expressing the pain she felt for the elder.

The woman shook her head, neck bone creaking. "Save the pity for yourself. You may end up like me, soon."

Marigold shut her eyes at the dreadful possibility. Her fingers clenched the rough, cold bars, and her lip quivered. "If that's what Father Creator wants, then...I'll manage somehow."

"Creator...you mean God? Ha, ha-ha-ha." The woman sounded amused, and Marigold looked across at her, confused. "How can you speak of God when we're in a place like this? It's His fault we're here, that I've been here for decades—wrapped up in misery with a blanket of pain and darkness for warmth.

How dare you speak of God."

Marigold shrunk back a little at the woman's anger; she had a lot to be angry about.

"I didn't mean to upset you…" Marigold replied timidly, sad she'd made the elder mad, but at the same time not liking how she blamed God. "Evil people put us in here, not God. But…but it'll be okay." She closed her eyes and breathed in. "My nonna always says that the body dies, but the soul lives forever."

The human woman remained silent, turning a hunched back to her.

Seeing she wasn't going to talk any further, Marigold moved back to her meager pile of hay.

The elder voice muttered, "Silly child thinks she's a grown-up, spouting big beliefs. We'll see how long that *faith* of yours lasts in this death-pit…*hehehe*."

Marigold tried to hide the sound of her sniffling tears in the dark. Papa…Nonna…would she ever see them again?

Three long days passed. She counted the meals. During the first day, not much happened. Several vempars passed through the dungeon, eyeing captives and choosing out a few who were then led away. Whispers among the cells said this happened when someone wealthy was looking to buy a slave, shopping around for one who would please them best. The only other time captives were taken from their cells was to collect their *essence*.

Marigold tried to keep calm, and thankfully no one came to her cell for either reason that day.

The jailor, a lanky, tall vempar with a rough-shaven jaw, fed the Reservoir captives—tossing bowls of "surprise soup" through horizontal slots in the door bars, just wide enough to fit food through, before latching the slot shut. When he came to Marigold's door and tossed the bowl through, she stood on wobbly knees to greet him, and attempted a cheerful smile, though her lips cracked and bled from the cold of last night. "Thank you for…" she said, trying not to flinch at the mysterious objects bobbing in the bowl, one of which looked like a frog, "…for the breakfast. I appreciate it," she finished.

The man's lazy-lidded gaze looked down at her, not expecting a captive to speak so politely. To beg for mercy or curse him, yes, but not this—and that's what Marigold wanted. "Oh? What a strange little thing you are. *Heh*." A ruthless grin spread his lips. "Pitiful newcomer. But you won't be gaining my favor that way." His throat chuckled. "After weeks of slop food, you'll be starving yourself. You'll be as wretched and despairing as the rest of this lot," he gestured and leered. "And then, you won't be able to recognize yourself—not even the hands in front of your face." He emphasized the last, twirling his hand, eyes gleaming as if looking forward to watching that happen.

Marigold plopped back down on the cell floor silently, and the jailor passed by to the next cell, dishing out more surprise soup. She peered down at the bowl, sniffed it, and almost puked. The stuff wasn't fit for any living creature's consumption.

Through the bars, she could see others swallowing and chewing bits and pieces anyway. She glanced once more at the bowl as a frog head and fish eyeballs floated to the surface. She pushed the dish aside, deciding to starve the day away.

Evening soup was no different…and neither were the next three days, and the following week. It wasn't going to change. Hunger finally drove her to attempt chewing some chunks that resembled gristle; she didn't dare to wonder what creature it came from.

She looked down at her thin frame, her rib bones that now

showed through. She wondered absently what her face must look like, starved, if she had a mirror. She sat on the damp floor, arms wrapped around her shins for warmth, wings wrapped around her back.

She continued giving a smile to every passerby, and to the lazy-eyed jailor, and kind words to the captives who were within hearing range. And she tried to keep the elder woman across from her encouraged, though the human pretended not to listen. Twice vempars had gathered *essence* from the woman that week—and that was fewer times than the captives left and right of them along the dungeon corridor. After each session, the elder was too weak to sit up, and Marigold watched and worried, offering bits of her own meager food gristle.

The emerald forest began to feel like a distant dream, a place that had only existed in her imagination. She could barely recall faces—Papa, Nonno and Nonna. Worry gnawed at her bones, and even more so when she noticed her wings were changing: Once so alive and shimmering green like a luna moth's, they were drooping lower and lower each day, their spark of life fading. She tried moving them, and they flapped weakly. Worry threatened to become anxiety inside her chest; the clammy, sullen atmosphere like an invisible weight that whispered she had no hope of ever seeing the blue sky and green grass again.

The gritty stone floor froze that night, and her ears filled with the scurrying patter of mice and rats. She missed the birds and their songs, the color of sunshine, the fresh scent of trees and loam.

Marigold counted the days by wrapping straws of hay around a cell bar. A growing part of her wanted to be selected as a slave, each time the vempars came searching through the cells. But it seemed nobody was interested in a gaunt faeryn child.

'Father Creator, please help me. I want to see the sunlight again. I feel like I'm fading away...' she prayed. *'But if you want to keep me*

here, please comfort me, please help my mind and keep the fears away.'

She tied another straw around the bar, and a sad thought hit her: *'I'll never see Papa or Nonna again.'* She couldn't picture her grandmother's face clearly in her mind anymore…

Face down, Marigold couldn't hold back the tears trickling down to the tip of her nose. She'd held out hope her family might still be alive after the attack, but deep inside she realized a part of her knew they weren't. She felt it; they were gone. Even if she managed to get free of this place, there was no home to go back to in the forest.

'Only in Heaven will I feel the grass beneath my feet again, and see…them,' she thought to herself.

A sudden scraping noise as the cell door opened lifted her head up from her tear-wet knees. Time for evening meal? But why open the door, and not the food slot? Was…were they planning on harvesting *essence* from her, already?

A jolt of panic shot up her spine and her heart beat fast in her ears. So soon they'd given up on selling her as a slave. Now she would be food. She silently hoped that having *essence* taken wouldn't hurt. She lifted her gaze to meet the vempar who stood waiting before her. It was the jailor.

He stared down his nose at her, a toothpick between his yellow teeth, lazy eyes evaluating her. At last he nodded, with what was almost a smile but so odd she couldn't quite be sure. "Yes, I think you'll fit the mold…after a bit of *fixing up*, that is."

She watched silently as he bent down on a knee, taking hold of the shackles that'd been digging into her ankles and wrists, unlocking them one by one. "You proved me wrong, y'know," he said. She blinked at him. His voice sounded different. "Even after two months, with no hope given to ya, you still keep a smile on that dirt-smeared face. Your faith hasn't wavered once."

His gaze met her at eye-level. "I'm not sure whether to

admire your spirit or think you a fool. Either way, I lost the bet. So…" Shackles now off, he lifted her frail body in his lanky arms, "I put in a good word for ya, and today you've been given a chance to get out of here," he said. "Seems a young lord's looking for a personal slave. Two others have been chosen as possible candidates besides you, though. It'll be up to the lad which of you he decides to take home." Carrying her out the cell, he added, "But anyway, let's get you looking fit for royalty!"

Marigold dangled in his arms, speechless. Then she glimpsed the old woman and quickly waved to her. "I won't stop praying for you, ever," she told her.

The woman closed her eyes, and for the first time Marigold saw her wrinkled lips turn up. "You proved me wrong too, I guess," her voice rasped. "If you can still trust God, then that leaves me with no excuse." A spark of life touched her weathered face.

Marigold smiled back at the sudden change, though a lump caught in her throat.

The jailor carried her off, and the old woman was gone from her sight.

<h1 style="text-align:center">3</h1>

It was a long walk through the cooled dungeon corridors and up the stairs from below ground, out the Reservoir building and into the light of day.

An early morning sky greeted Marigold with its rosy warmth, refreshing her spirit, washing the dungeon's darkness away. She took in the wide expanse of blue for as long as she could, hoping this wouldn't be her last time seeing it, until they entered a fanciful house which sat not far from the Reservoir.

"This here's the prepping place for soon-to-be-sold slaves," said the jailor. "We have to make ya look nice, for when buyers come and evaluate."

Inside, he led her to a room where a wide assortment of dresses, hairbrushes, vials of makeup and other beauty products cluttered the closet and dressers.

"I know this isn't the kind of life you imagined for yourself, but serving the Dragonsbane House might not be so bad."

Was he trying to reassure her? Him, of all people?

"A bit lonesome and harsh, with people telling you what to do day-in and day-out, but…it's better than being locked away as food supply." He set her down on a cushioned stool which rotated. "Remember: be respectful, and look no one in the eye. Those upper-class types like a slave to be obedient and meek."

As he straightened from setting her down, a woman came bustling in, wearing the simple dress of a hired servant. When her eyes came to rest on Marigold, they grew wide as saucers, and a gasp escaped her O-shaped mouth. "What on eartha…this child looks more bedraggled and frayed than a cleaning rag!" Her fury turned on the jailor. "What am I supposed to do with *this*?" She gestured at all of her. "It's no ordinary businessman or shop keeper coming by—it's His Grace of House Dragonsbane! Both he *and* his son. You dense nitwit!"

Marigold made herself small in the chair. Exactly how bad was her appearance? She shifted to peer in the mirror on the wall across from her, and flinched at the starving, filthy and bruised body that was hers.

"See? Even she's afraid at the sight of herself!"

The jailor's lazy eyelids watched the woman servant, waiting for her tirade to end, and once it had, he simply gave a shrug. "A person's got to do the best they can with what they've got. C'mon, woman, it shouldn't be *that* difficult to get her looking pretty."

The woman shook a fist in his face, "*Yooou*— If the Dragonsbanes make a complaint, it'll be *your* head on the line, y'hear?"

The corners of his lips twitched. "Best you start working your magic on the little lady, then, before they get here," he said.

And then he dashed off before she could holler any more.

The woman made an angry *tsk* sound.

The first step in the beautifying process was Healing: Marigold sat stiffly, feeling a channel of icy energy seep into her skin beneath the woman's hand as it rested roughly across her bruised ankles, Healing the blemishes away. Repeating the process wherever she had damage.

Next step, a bath: Marigold tried not to yelp as the vempar woman scrubbed her down viciously—getting off every speck of dirt and dry skin until she was pink as a strawberry.

Next, the hair: Marigold sat eating a loaf of bread with sliced cheese over a small table as the woman worked, since her stomach wouldn't stop growling and annoying her. She stayed put in a rotating chair while the woman yanked and brushed and combed at her hair, only stopping once the blonde colors shimmered and gleamed like molten honey. Then she set about weaving it into an intricate, thick braid with loose and curled strands falling about Marigold's cheeks, framing her petite face.

Next, makeup: Marigold had to keep her eyelids shut tight the entire time as the woman dabbed and brushed and tweezed speedily. After that, the final step was dressing. The servant made her stand while she held up outfit after outfit, racing to decide which color and what style looked best and could fit her wings through.

Her wings... Marigold held in a painful sigh, barely able to look at them. Nonna had once said that a faeryn's wings were connected to their spirit: *"A free spirit has wings to soar the dawn sky, but a spirit held captive can no longer take flight."*

"Sit up straight!" The woman's curt command made her jolt. She kept glancing at the clock above the fireplace mantle. "The Dragonsbanes are almost here..." she murmured.

Making up her mind at last, the servant stuffed Marigold into a layered satin and silk green dress, green as a pond, bringing out the mint color in her eyes, lace ruffles down the bodice, the neck V-shaped with a short collar, sleeves lightly puffed and short, paired with white leather gloves that rose to her elbows. She stuffed her feet in tan shoe-boots, then tied a green ribbon bow at the end of her braided hair, and a second bow just above the right ear behind her bangs.

Altogether, in the mirror Marigold looked pretty as a painting. She let herself smile a little. She still preferred the feel of soft faeryn clothing, but this was beautiful too.

The servant steered her by the shoulders into a large sitting room of fine décor, two other captive girls already present there, fully beautified and waiting. They would be inspected and evaluated here by the coming family.

The jailor, before making his way back outdoors to the Reservoir, caught sight of her. The line of his mouth turned up. "Keep your cool, little lady, and don't forget my advice!" he said.

The woman servant shooed him out the door, and he managed a wink before disappearing from sight. Marigold swallowed hard, fearful butterflies filling her stomach with every passing second.

Exactly how important was this noble family? What if she made a mistake? What if the prettier girls standing beside her— who looked well fed, not bony and gaunt like her—what if the buyer liked one of *them* more? She glanced sidelong at them. Both were human, and a year or so older than her. Perspiration dampened her forehead.

But what was meant to be would be, and what wasn't would not. Simple as that, she had to remind herself. No need to stress.

She sucked in a breath. And besides, these girls needed a home too. She didn't want them to end up in the cold dungeons she just came from.

So, no matter what the outcome today, she'd be okay with it.

The creak of doors opening cut off all train of thought.

She could hear the woman servant greeting people. And a second, gruff male voice spoke, "As the Reservoir's caretaker, I assure you that only the finest of slaves have been brought out for your selection, Your Grace."

The caretaker—whom she'd never seen before—and the woman servant welcomed the guests indoors, with all the grandeur they could muster. Marigold listened to the entourage of footsteps entering the main doors. The two girls beside her were breathing hard through their noses, but keeping expressionless despite beads of sweat, their gazes staring down at the floor before their pretty shoes.

After a second's hesitation, she quickly did the same, but only after catching a glimpse of an exquisitely dressed lady—her hair oddly wrapped up in the shape of a cat?—and a stoic lord, both making their way toward the sitting room with an escort of two guards and three servants. The caretaker and woman servant guided the group, leading the way and all the while boasting about their finest young slaves available in Draethvyle. They strategically added in ego-boosting words of "What an honor it is to meet you, Your Graces. We are truly blessed by your presence," and such.

Marigold spotted a young boy around her age: He strode nonchalantly alongside the lady, dressed in a fine suit and cravat, his pearl-gray hair combed in a swoop toward the right side of his face. His sour expression was far from elegant though, declaring he would rather be anywhere else.

She quickly lowered her head, giving a curtsy when the two human girls did so. The family of House Dragonsbane came to a stop within the elegant sitting room, eyeing what candidates the Reservoir had on display for them.

She could feel their intense gazes, examining each of them, and suddenly knew how a lungofante must feel when faeryn evaluated them before purchase. Beneath the white gloves, her hands trembled, and she clenched them tighter together.

"As you see, we've brought out nothing but the best of young girls in stock," the caretaker said, indicating all three with an arm sweep, full of pride. Thankfully he was too distracted to notice Marigold's gaunt frame beneath the dress and makeup.

The nobleman looked unimpressed, and the lady fanned herself with a feather fan in thought.

With a worried swallow, the caretaker added that these were merely "today's finest," and that if the young lord wasn't pleased with any of *these*, the caretaker would have "tomorrow's finest" delivered specially to Dragonsbane Mansion for evaluation.

Lord Dragonsbane remained expressionless as stone, making the caretaker sweat and fidget in his shoes even more. The woman servant, off to the side, looked nearly sick, probably wishing she hadn't listened to the jailor and added such a gaunt-looking faeryn to the stock.

"Do that, then," Lord Dragonsbane said with an edge. "Send us a better stock tomorrow."

Marigold's heart fell… The chance at a life seeing the blue sky overhead was gone.

"Now now, my darling Renald," Lady Dragonsbane said, waving her fan, full pouting lips turned up in what she clearly believed was a cute smile. "Don't rush off just yet! This is for Hercule to decide. It's *his* birthday present, not yours."

Lord Renald turned his chin with a disapproving snort.

The lady tried to bend at the waist against her tight dress to speak in Hercule's ear, "Go on, my darling silver duckling. Is there one among these you fancy? The human with brown curls is a pretty little thing, yes?"

Hercule huffed, then finally turned his head to have a glance at each candidate. The girls stood still, eyes lowered before him, he noted. No, wait. That one faeryn just looked at him—flicking her mint-green eyes up just enough to see his face before quickly lowering again. Her cheeks were coloring now, knowing she'd been caught in the act.

Hercule's gaze lingered. There was something about her, a defiance that felt almost refreshing. Faeryn were unusual creatures to look at: with their long, pointed ears sticking out to either side, hair of mixed colors, and freckled patches on their skin, and the way their pupils weren't black but instead a darker shade of their irises. This girl's skin was the color of angel-cake, with her mottled skin spots colored honey. He supposed it was pretty in an artistic sort of way. Her hair was a fascinating mix of honey, flaxen, and amber streaks.

He really didn't want another slave in the mansion, another person catering to him, bowing and asking if he needed anything, acting as if they cared when it was all lies. Nobody truly cared; it was money that ruled everything. Having a personal slave attendant would make his life worse, some kid his age tagging along, glued to his heels wherever he went… The thought sparked anger inside him.

But Father and Mother were insistent. He had no choice but to do as they pleased and choose someone, whether it be now or later. He may as well choose and get this over with now. And besides, he felt strangely drawn to the blonde faeryn with sagging wings.

"Her." Hercule indicated with a chin nod. "That blonde faeryn with the braid."

Marigold stood motionless, her heart leaping, though she could see the crestfallen faces of the other two girls.

Lady Dragonsbanc made a surprised sound, eyebrows tilted inward, and she surveyed Marigold with distaste. "Her? Really?

But—but the other two are so pretty! Not frail and bony and…"

A smirk touched Hercule's lips. "Then I choose her all the more," he said. "She'll gain weight once she's fed."

The lady puckered, pouting like a child, but she *had* said this was Hercule's decision. "V-very well, then! As long as you're certain, darling."

Hercule glanced sideways up at his father. The line of Lord Renald's mouth pressed tighter. Hercule quickly spoke before he could: "She'll be made to fit the part, Mother, don't fret. Besides, I can't afford to waste more valuable time picking and choosing. A nobleson has better things to do! Like my piano lessons beginning soon." He brushed pearly gray bangs back from his forehead, turning away with his chin held high regally, and then he marched out the room before anything more could be said. "Let the servants back home tidy the faeryn up and teach her properly!"

Marigold stared. This boy was as haughty as a prince and expected his will to be carried out without argument.

Amusement touched the edges of Lord Renald's lips. He turned away as well, ordering over a shoulder as he left, "You heard my son. Send for one of your carriages and have the slave brought to the mansion. I will tolerate no delays."

The caretaker and servants jumped at his stern command, then quickly bowed and curtsied.

As soon as the noble family were outside and getting into their grand motor carriage, both the caretaker and a female faeryn slave—in her late thirties, who'd been left behind by the Dragonsbanes to see the orders carried out—hurried Marigold to the back of the house, through a back door and into a yard of parked carriages.

Marigold barely had a chance to look back at the woman and two girls, all of whom had stunned looks on their faces, one of them carefully waving farewell.

4

Dragonsbane Mansion was the grandest thing that Marigold could ever have imagined, the architecture and style of it all so foreign from anything in the forest villages. Overwhelmed as she felt by this new world, she was also fascinated.

The drive circled round a thing called a fountain, with the proud statue of a lady slaying a dragon at its center. She gawked as the motor carriage rumbled to a stop——the carriage device itself a strange wonder to her——and a footman opened the door to let her out. The man eyed her coolly, as did the other servants, as she entered the mansion not through the grand door bearing the Dragonsbane crest, but through a modest side door meant for servants.

The head butler led her over, and left her to the vempar housekeeper—the woman who oversaw the female servants and slaves. Before Marigold had a chance to curtsy, the housekeeper began spouting all the rules at her: "Act properly, sit up straight, and keep your head and eyes lowered, remain standing unless given permission, do any and every task the lord, lady, or young lord says immediately, and no meals allowed outside the servants' quarters—*it's improper for slaves to be seen eating*—and you can only eat after the Dragonsbanes have finished their meal."

Marigold blinked up at her. The list went on and on, but that was as much as Marigold's befuddled brain could retain.

It was late afternoon by the time the housekeeper had her dressed in a plain gray serving gown and apron, and the pretty outfit from the sellers tucked away. Marigold was about to be led down to the kitchens and clean dishes, when a servant came and whispered in the housekeeper's ear.

"Milord Hercule has just sent for you, it seems." The housekeeper looked down her nose at Marigold. "And that means you run with all haste to see what it is he wants, little chickpea faeryn. You're his personal slave—so when he calls, you answer. Now get your bony backside moving!" She shoved roughly at her back. "Up the stairs and to the left!"

Marigold jumped and hurried up the servants' staircase before the woman could snap a towel on her rump, and she reached the safety of the floor above.

She tiptoed through the left hallway, glimpsing tapestries and curious vases as she went, trying to calm the bundle of nerves inside her. Every window showed the sky, and she felt tempted to open them and let the fresh air in. What was this Hercule like? Could they become friends? It'd be nice to have someone to talk to in this grand, lonely house.

Lord Hercule's quarters, when she finally found them after

peeking inside every door, were a series of rooms—apparently wealthy vempars needed more than one.

Why had he picked her? She very much wanted to ask. The boy's father seemed as hard as an unmovable mountain, but hopefully his son would be kinder. It'd be so much fun to run about the mansion and go on excursions with a friend!

A light tap echoed from Hercule's bedroom door. Hercule raised his chin from adjusting his shirt collar in the mirror. "Come in, already!"

The honey-blonde faeryn entered, closing the door behind her. Her long ears twitched. She looked confused, like she wasn't sure if she ought to curtsy or offer a smile or simply stare at the floor. Hercule heaved a disgruntled sigh. "You were supposed to wait in the parlor."

The slave looked up, as if concerned she'd already messed up on her first day of the job. "What's a parlor?" she whispered to herself.

Hercule rubbed his head against an oncoming headache.

Marigold met his eyes, close enough this time to see their liquid gold color, with flecks of amber and burnt gold, black pupils slightly vertical. The name Dragonsbane suited his bloodline well. She suddenly realized that she was breaking the rules by staring at him, and she blushed, looking away and fumbling for words—or was she allowed to speak yet? "...Uh...*ehm*..."

"I called you here," Hercule spoke with impatience, "so that I could state what is to be expected of you. But let me make one thing clear, first." He faced her, with the same cold arrogance that everyone in this mansion seemed to have. "I don't want you," he said bluntly.

Marigold kept frozen to the spot.

"I don't even *need* you, except my father insists that I have a personal slave attendant," he said distastefully. "Don't expect any special treatment or favors from me, nor silly ideas about friendship. You're just a slave that I have to put up with. Understand?"

Marigold's lower lip quivered, but she kept her back stiff and expression blank.

Once Hercule seemed satisfied that she understood, he turned to a table beside the mirror, several books across it. "Your duties are basically to follow me wherever I go. Carry things—like these books, or my coat, or anything I may want. You'll also keep track of my daily schedule, serve my meals, provide snacks I want throughout the day, and serve tea at teatime." He paused, squinting at her. "Is this overloading your tiny faeryn brain? I'll put it in *simpler* terms: Do you know what an assistant is? Because that's what you are—and more to the extreme, since you're a slave. They title the job *personal attendant*, but it's the same thing."

He brushed his hair back with a hand. "I don't like this any more than you do. I hate the idea of having somebody follow me around, *tch*! There's no need for it here at home, so I'll have you help the other slaves with their chores when you aren't assisting me. They'll probably make you clean these rooms daily, and do the laundry..." He frowned, as if disturbed by something. "Leave the private things alone. A person should be responsible for his own undergarments," he said. "I don't care if other nobles are fine with having people touch their underwear. I'm not!"

He turned his nose up, arms folded haughtily. "Anyway, there'd better not be a speck of dust in my room after you clean, you hear me? Nor a wrinkle on my shirts when you put them away. They're more expensive than anything a lowly maggot like you could imagine—all of my things are, and don't you forget it."

Marigold remained stoic faced.

"You look too soft and weak," he said with a huff. "Toughen up. I don't take pity on the weak."

"Is there anything you need me to do for you right now, milord?" she asked.

Hercule lowered his chin, startled by her soft-feather voice. Her luna moth wings drooped like leaves down her back. Hercule thought, *'Why is it every faeryn I see has their wings wilted down like that?'* Faeryn were supposed to be able to fly with those, and yet he'd never seen one flying.

Marigold almost took a step back when Hercule grabbed her shoulders. "M-milord?" she stuttered.

"There's one more thing I'm supposed to do," he said. "Father says I'm to place a Mark on you; it's customary of ownership, and a necessity. Stop shaking like a leaf!" he commanded, sounding annoyed. "You belong to me. Be grateful I didn't choose to use you as a *pet* instead."

There, he thought, that should be enough to frighten the girl and keep her in line.

While in the dungeon, Marigold had heard whispers about *pets*: people treated less like a slave and more like a prized source of *essence*. Her shaking knees nearly gave out.

Holding her stiffly by the shoulders, Hercule's face lowered to the side of her neck. She wanted to run. Small tears welled at the corners of her vision.

'I was brought here for a reason. There must be a reason! I won't back down, not now,' she told herself, while feeling the brush of lips on her neck. Her eyelids squeezed shut. Every inch of her tensed as fangs pierced through skin.

"You can open your eyes," a very annoyed voice told her. Marigold did, a tiny bit, and saw Hercule standing there, holding a stack of books, waiting. "Don't tell me I chose a lazy bum for a slave." He rolled his eyes. "All I did was put a slave-bond Mark on you. You do know what that is, right? It means you can't run away—I can always track you down—and you have to do what I tell you. It also shows that you're *my* property, so other people can't go stealing you away."

Marigold gingerly touched the side of her neck but couldn't feel anything. Only by looking in a mirror did she see the ink-like Mark in the elaborate shape of a dragon's wing there. Hercule huffed and tossed the books at her. She whirled, trying to catch the lot.

Turning sharply on the heels of his polished brown shoes, Hercule ordered, "Follow me. And no lagging behind!"

She hurried after him, balancing the heavy books in her frail, clumsy arms.

The books were then deposited sloppily on the wide table in Hercule's study room, where she bobbed a curtsy to the vempar tutor already there, waiting for Hercule's signal that he was ready to begin lessons.

The nobleson shooed her away to wait outside the door. "I'll explain this once," Hercule told her. "Every school day, you're to stand out here, waiting in case I need refreshments—I must keep well hydrated and fed for my brain to function at its best. Learning takes great concentration! Not something I'd expect a maggot to understand.

"Eleven o'clock is teatime. Bring the *earl heavensing* tea. And, whatever you do, don't forget the shortbread cookies!" he emphasized, before shutting the door in her face.

Marigold stared at the mahogany wood panels for a long moment, her long ears catching the tutor's muffled words begin a lesson on ancient literature. Her mouth puckered.

"Those must be some delicious cookies…"

Leaning against the wall beside the door, which was ornamented with patterned paper of cream and reds, her head nodded back as fatigue lulled her to sleep. A huge clock—one of many about the mansion—stood tall resembling a tree, with a perched dragon on top. It stood where the hallway met a balcony overlooking the grand staircase. Clocks weren't foreign to her, but it still looked impressive. She woke when the big artifact bonged.

It was five minutes 'til eleven… Aah! Teatime! Was she supposed to go fix it? But Hercule had said to remain at the door. Maybe someone would come hand it to her? She glanced about, but no one was around. *Eek*, she was in trouble. "I have to get it myself!" she decided and dashed down the staircase that was meant for aristocrats, unsure of the way to the kitchen. The mansion was worse than a forest to get lost in, with no north-growing lichens to guide her way!

She wandered in a hurry, keeping an eye out for any servants' doors—the only difference seeming to be that they weren't as fanciful. Finally she spotted one, and dashed to reach it before anyone saw her.

But instead of reaching the door, she bumped into someone. "*Ai*, excuse me, I'm sorry!" She looked up instinctively, before remembering the rule and quickly looking down. The vempar appeared well dressed, perhaps a visiting guest. Tall, with skin the shade of a thunderstorm, dark hair combed back in a low ponytail. His gaze narrowed down at her briefly, as if spotting a fly, before dismissing the faeryn's presence.

Close behind him came Lord Dragonsbane, escorting this important guest, whoever he was, until she'd interrupted. Marigold didn't have to see the noble's face to feel the outrage and embarrassment seeping from him, as if she had done the most offensive thing in the world. She started shaking, bony knees clacking together.

"What is this?" Lord Dragonsbane grabbed her forearm, pulling the slave clear of his guest, releasing her with a toss that hit her back against the wall. She tried to speak and apologize, but he raged, "Don't talk back to me! Learn your place, slave. I will not tolerate such behavior. If you were mine, I'd have you whipped!"

Marigold flinched.

He continued, "I'll let my son do the punishing. He should gain some experience in learning how to handle unruly, ignorant slaves."

The head butler appeared around the corner, drawn in by the commotion. Seeing that Marigold was the cause, his eyes nearly bugged out of his blond head. He rushed in and grabbed her arm, pulling her away from the noble's wrath and over to the servants' door. "Do not trouble yourself, Your Grace," he said quickly. "Allow me to deal with this matter for you." Being a vempar with a high servant's status, he could speak and take matters into his own hands.

Shoved through the door, Marigold could hear the noble's apologies toward his guest: "I sincerely apologize, Sir Swornyte. It was purchased just this morning and doesn't yet know the ways of..."

The voices faded as the door closed.

It. She was nothing more than a *thing.*

"Foolish child!" the head butler muttered, steering her down the narrow staircase and corridor to the kitchens beneath the mansion. His hair came down in a single, thin braid, swaying over his shoulder. "It's the little lord's teatime, isn't it?" he said. It wasn't a question, but she nodded meekly.

"You're late!" barked the head maid as they reached the kitchen. "I had to go and fix this myself, after serving Lady Chatsalott hers. Why? Because I realized *you* weren't going to, you lazy twig! Everybody's busy doing *their* job, preparing midday meals, except you." The woman stomped, mad as a hornet. "Chickpea, it's *your* duty to serve the young lord now— not *ours!*" She slapped Marigold's cheek, leaving a narrow cut from a fingernail. "You fix and serve his tea from now on, hear me? Or I promise you, I'll—"

The head butler waved a white-gloved hand for the woman to simmer down a notch. "The child is new. She hasn't been raised to serve nobility, or anyone, for that matter. Honestly, I don't know why she was chosen."

"A real mistake, that was!" the head maid said sharply. The butler's frown tightened. She neither noticed nor cared, shoving a fine porcelain tea set on a tray into Marigold's hands. "Off with you! Now-now-now!" She clapped.

Marigold backed up, unsure which way to run, until the butler's finger tapped her shoulder. She craned her neck as his height loomed over her short stature. "I'll show you the proper servants' way back. Come," he said. She had the feeling that when he'd freed her of Lord Dragonsbane's grasp, he'd saved her from something terrible. Maybe this butler wasn't such a bad person.

By the time Marigold reached the study room door, it was six minutes past eleven. "There you are!" Hercule frowned as she entered and set the tray on a little side table. Her head lowered further, trying to shrink like a turtle in its shell. "I can't believe this. No slave has ever been late serving tea before."

Hercule rose from the open book before him, pointing a finger at the gilded clock on a shelf. "Look! Do you see that? Do you *see* what time it is? *Tch!*" He moved over to the tray, not allowing her the chance to poor the tea but impatiently doing it himself. "I don't know why I picked you," he muttered, head shaking. "First day on the job, and you make a fine mess of everything, like a wild pup in a parlor. If this keeps up, I'll be exchanging you for something better." Hercule flipped his bangs, nose in the air. "That's what happens with shoes that don't fit right, you know. You exchange them for ones that do." He shooed her with his hand, "Go back outside."

Marigold chewed her lip, desperately trying to hold in tears that wanted to flow free. She turned with a curtsy and went out the door. It was hard enough being yelled at by the lord, then slapped by a maid, and now *this*. There was no pity in those cold, golden eyes.

And the day wasn't over yet. After Hercule finished with his lessons, Lord Dragonsbane sent to have a talk with him. An hour later found Marigold in the sitting room of Hercule's quarters, standing before the young nobleson as he stated to her her wrong doings.

"Father says slaves need strict guidelines and must be taught how to behave." Hercule's jaw clenched for one moment. "I'm supposed—" He stopped, then began again. "As your master, I have to punish you. It's a waste of my valuable time, but it has to be done." He hardened his expression.

Marigold wondered *what* sort of punishment, when stings like a whip suddenly struck her legs and back.

She stumbled. Nothing visible was hitting her, yet red welts blossomed across her skin. The whip sensation struck again and again, and the tears she'd held back from before now dripped down her cheeks.

"This is part of the slave-bond, the Mark on your neck. It lets me punish you with pain," said Hercule, pointing at her. "I'll be lenient this time. But the next…I'll make it so you won't be able to sleep for a week."

His hand dropped and the whip stings ceased. The welts still burned beneath her clothes. Hercule left her there, saying he wanted to spend the rest of the day alone.

Good. She wanted to be alone too.

It took close to an hour before Marigold felt stable enough to stand on her scrawny, now red marked legs. She made her way over to the bathroom, and there cleaned and wrapped bandages around her legs and some of her back. She did it quickly, before anyone could find and punish her for using the nobleson's bathroom and things.

Sunset came, and with it dinnertime. Marigold stood at the dining table behind Hercule's chair, refilling his cup and plate when he demanded. The lord and lady's attendants did the same for them. Before eating, Lord Dragonsbane recited a simple prayer.

'Prayer?' thought Marigold. How dare such cruel and insensitive people like them pray! Whatever they claimed to believe, their actions were going against God's will. And it set her blood boiling.

She tried to hide her emotions, until dinner finally ended, then she followed Hercule upstairs to his quarters. The sky beyond the bedroom windows glowed with the subdued shades of twilight, and the first stars emerged. The dragon-eyed boy pointed to a makeshift pallet laid out on the floor of the bathroom, back in a corner. "That's where you're to sleep. Don't snore, or I'll make you sleep outside in the cold."

Staring down at the pitiful excuse for a bed, something inside Marigold snapped. Her hands squeezed together and one foot stomped on the silk carpeted floor. Hercule turned at the noise, a question in his haughty eyebrows.

"How can you pray to God, when you ignore the very things He teaches?"

Hercule blinked, surprised at the sudden outburst, then gave her a haughty glare. "If you're referring to slaves, many people in the Bible had slaves, and punished them when they deserved it."

She shook her head fiercely, "Not like this! *'Love your neighbor as yourself.'* You're supposed to value our lives. We have the same worth as you."

"*Hmph.*" He stared down his nose at her. "Are you sure about that?"

Her fists clenched harder. "Stop praying! You're not a follower of God, so stop pretending!"

Hercule almost looked amused for a moment, then said, "I *am* a follower. Though my parents aren't. They follow the Church of Draeth and its three goddesses."

He chuckled at the surprised look on her face. "Yes, I believe in God—and I don't have to be a good person."

She flinched at the dark face he made.

"I can do whatever I want, I can act however I want, and it won't change the fact that I'll go to Heaven."

His lips smirked at her burning anger.

"Do you even believe you're a sinner in need of saving?" she confronted him.

He shrugged carelessly. "Sure, we all do mean and bad things. But, so what? God's Son paid the price for all of that. Now I'm free to be how I want."

"No." She cooled her tone. "If you don't care about God and His teachings, then He won't care about *you*. Father God won't help you when you need it or give you any more blessings."

"Blessings?" Hercule turned, spreading his arms wide to encompass the room, the mansion and everything grand around him, laughter on his lips. "Look at all the blessings God's given me. Look! And it won't end here—no, no. Every day of my life, I'll have the full wealth of House Dragonsbane, and even more so when I take over as the High Seat of the House! You're just jealous of me, maggot, admit it. Jealous I can act how I want and get what I want."

The anger in Marigold suddenly diminished, and it caught him off-guard. "No...I pity you. There's so much you don't have," she said. "True faith shows through our actions. How we behave shows what we really believe. You should read *James 2* and *Galatians 5:22*."

Her footsteps moved toward the small, lumpy pallet in the bathroom. "If you're a true follower of God, He *will* punish you one day, just like a parent punishes their child." She turned. "And if He doesn't, that means He doesn't consider you family—and He doesn't love you."

Hercule's gaze trailed after her. Then he snorted, turning his nose away. He muttered to himself as he changed into silk pajamas, not bothering to command her to put away his clothes.

"...Stupid faeryn," he muttered into his pillow.

Over the next several weeks, Hercule made it his mission to get Marigold into as much trouble as possible: Bumping a table she was cleaning so that the rare vase fell off and shattered. Taking things out of the laundry basket and pretending she'd lost his expensive cravats because of her maggot-sized brain. Making a tray of eleven o'clock teatime snack tilt off the desk— porcelain cups and valuable tea wasted on the floor.

He blamed her when he got a low score on a test, claiming she'd interrupted his studies. Blamed her for pushing him into the pond, when really he'd gone for a swim in spite of Father's rule about "looking presentable at all times"—guests had been visiting, and they saw his drenched state.

The list of things went on, and he neither noticed nor cared how Marigold suffered. She was serving her purpose, as far as he was concerned. It was nice to have someone else suffer in this mansion besides himself.

5

I wish I had listened to her… I wish I had taken heed of God's warning… But selfishness is a sin that blinds you to all else.

House Dragonsbane ruled the silk industry in the Vemparic Kingdom. There wasn't one place, even internationally, where silk wasn't sold in some form. As the Head of the House, Father often traveled and made inspections of the various silk factories and facilities, ensuring that all was running smoothly and efficiently—something that Father said was very important for the owner of any product to do.

"Inspect your wares. Otherwise, problems may arise when you least expect them."

Today, Father made plans to travel to the capital of Higashi, the eastern lands, where the largest facilities and growing fields of the precious silkworm were located. This time, he agreed to let Hercule come along and see how things were managed, and Hercule was secretly excited.

Being the nobleson's personal slave attendant, Marigold was tagging along for the journey. She quietly enjoyed the long ride in the black-and-gold painted motor carriage, following the dirt-flattened road which led from Draethvyle into the country. The oilpowder engine of the sturdy yet stylish carriage rumbled. An escort of guards and three Draevs rode on bladecycles around them. Instead of taking the travel-tram, Lord Renald wanted his motor carriage to use while in Higashi.

The carriage was comfortable enough to fit eight inside, without anybody too close, and a small table folded up when not in use. Renald, Chatsalott and Hercule sat on one side, the staff and slave on the other. The lady-in-waiting continuously fanned Lady Dragonsbane across from her, while Lord Renald discussed with his head butler and valet a list of things that would need doing once they arrived. The head butler's name was Lynk, the same man who had helped Marigold on her first day. She glanced at Hercule, seated opposite her, then continued gazing out the window at the passing countryside landscape.

Hercule looked bored to death, staring blankly at the clouds. She would've offered to play a game, except she'd probably get yelled at.

After a while, Butler Lynk, beside her, made some quiet conversation to entertain her when Renald was finished. With other conversations going on around them, their quiet voices went unnoticed. Butler Lynk seemed kinder than the other House servants. Maybe he was used to being around slaves, so it didn't bother his pride much conversing with them.

Marigold realized she was the only non-vempar on the trip. Lynk, the valet, and lady-in-waiting were all vempars of high society—not as high as nobles, but above middle-class. Having a high-ranking job in a Noble House was good for raising one's status in society. Serving gave them connections and favor from the most powerful people in Draeth.

There was a big difference between servants and slaves: Servants were vempars, who received payment for their service, and weren't given a horrid Mark. And they made up the higher positions in the House. Lynk quietly explained these things to her.

She gazed with longing out the window at the passing trees, wishing to return to the forest, even if there'd be an empty home waiting for her. At least there were no stupid rules and bullying and punishments there...

They paused their journey and spent the night at a small village—the inn there surprisingly classy, and all meals fresh from the farms. Far into the next travel day, their entourage finally arrived at Higashi, and Marigold's eyes widened with awe.

The landscape was broken by mountains, but they were more like pinnacles and swords of rock rising into the sky, trees scattered about their narrow ledges and the tops of their pointed heads. They passed between the soaring pinnacles and onto rolling hills, which dipped into a valley. The woods had unusual trees called *bamboo*; and many fields and terraced hills held pools of water used for growing rice, Lynk told her. People waded through knee-high water, wearing wide conical straw hats. She smiled, wanting one of those hats.

The capital, Akatsuki, sat nestled in a coastal valley, extending out into a canal-like bay on the east side, which eventually connected to the sea. Canoe-like boats of all sizes rowed about its salty waters, bringing in fish, crabs and other treasures. The silkworm farming fields were located among the green hills and cultivated trees to the north.

Marigold and Hercule both stared, openly amazed at the foreign culture, a separate world all its own. There was much profit to be made in the eastern land, but only a handful of vempar merchants were allowed in by the ruling kitsune dynasty to distribute eastern items to the rest of the world, and vise-versa. Mostly the silk industry and slavemasters made big profit, having established trading deals. Higashi wasn't a strong country, and they were well aware of the power of their neighbor, the Vemparic Kingdom, and wanted to keep good relations with them.

The carriage drove past a female kitsune. The humanoid lady had furry ears like a fox, matching furry feet and a fluffy fox tail. Her brown eyes were slanted, as she briefly met Marigold's gaze. Colorful robes swayed in the breeze around her, held by a waist tie.

Many kitsune in the city they passed looked poor, and yet the building structures were freshly painted in bright colors as if new—rust-red, white, and greens—and they soared several stories high, tiered like cakes, with curving roofs.

Servants shuffled the Dragonsbanes' luggage inside a grand inn of soaring tiered, green roofs. Depictions of snake-like dragons, cranes and flowers decorated everything as Marigold explored about.

Lord Dragonsbane didn't waste time; he and the valet set off to begin inspections of the silkworm farming fields nearby. Hercule hurried to go with him. But when Marigold followed him out the inn, the boy turned. "This is Dragonsbane business," he told her. "It's nothing to do with a slave. I won't need you there. But if you're bored, you can have my tea ready for when I return."

Marigold's lips puckered bitterly. Hercule knew she wanted to explore the land and see the silkworms. He smirked over his shoulder, and the faeryn stood there on the inn's front steps watching them climb into the motor carriage and set off, some guards and a Draev following—the rest remained with Lady Chatsalott. The woman was already planning to use this trip as a big shopping spree.

Butler Lynk appeared. "Marigold, would you like to come with me and assist our lady with her shopping?"

Marigold turned, looking up at his light smile.

"If there's one thing in this world I cannot stand, it's the disappointed face of a child," the vempar admitted, then bent down to her long ear and whispered, "Maybe we can secretly get you one of those *hats*."

Marigold resisted the urge to jump excitedly and nodded eagerly instead.

Hercule strolled the sloping fields in the late afternoon sun. Low trees grew in neat rows, their branches bustling with silkworms that wove white threads about the leaves. Sunset colored the city's unusual rooftops and the peaks of the sharp mountains surrounding them.

Father finished grilling the manager of the farm fields about improvements, while Hercule observed and listened. All that talk about business bored him though. It was more fun holding the soft silkworms in his palm and watching them spin threads like a spider—so fascinating how the stuff could be transformed and made into clothing!

Hercule yawned, finally tired out and glad once they returned to the inn and ate a dinner of foreign cuisine: sushi, grilled fish, unusual noodle dishes, and dumplings with different fillings. Unusual, but delicious enough.

Marigold enjoyed the meal when it was the servants' turn to eat. Lady Chatsalott had a mountain of bags from her shopping spree to put away: of local fabrics, exotic perfumes, teas, jewelry, and more. Poor Butler Lynk had had a rough time carrying the load, and now he was trying to figure out where to store it all.

Marigold held in a secret smile. Hidden in her traveling bag was one of the conical straw hats and a colorful paper umbrella Lynk had bought for her.

In the bedroom she shared with the lady-in-waiting, Marigold opened the sliding door and peeked out into the night. The landscape was peaceful and serenaded by pet crickets singing from little bamboo cages. The after dark bustling of the streets was blocked out by the inn's wall and the rise of a slope, allowing guests an undisturbed sleep. She yawned and lay down on the firm pallet bed, pretending the crickets were those of her forest home.

Hercule shifted, tossing and turning restlessly on the firm *futon* bed, so low it made him feel like he was sleeping on the floor. With a frustrated grunt, he hauled himself off.

The air felt warm beyond the sliding paper window. He tied on a silk robe and tiptoed through the sliding door and out into the night.

He moved, careful not to make a sound until he was well clear of the closed door. The full moon cast light and shadow over the rooftops and into a quaint area behind the inn: a courtyard of grass and a perfectly round pond, with a single willow tree beside it, its thin leaves shifting in the breeze. Pink lotus flowers bobbed just above the surface, the moon's reflection rippling across the waters. Beyond the area, a stand of bamboo trees led back into a forest, and he wondered what sort of creatures might stir in the darkness out there.

He watched the moon, then his reflection in the pond, when a sound like chiming bells began softly from the trees.

His eyes scanned about for the source, as the breeze rustled leaves and jostled his bangs back from his face. The breeze grew into a swirling wind, and he had to raise a hand, shielding his eyes. The chiming increased with the wind.

"What is this?" he murmured, squinting.

A loud chime sounded, and then everything went still. All fell silent.

Hercule frantically looked about.

But there was nothing to be seen.

"It's probably just a string of bells tied somewhere..." he reassured himself.

He was about to hurry back indoors, when he glimpsed movement, and halted. A figure cloaked in red stepped out from the bamboo woods: a woman, with pale green skin, and pale pink hair spilling long and wavy around her. Tiny silver bells threaded through narrow braids, showering her tresses. They chimed with her every move.

Hercule started. She was a goblin. A lone traveler, or else she'd made this foreign land her home. Either way, she had no right to be wandering about behind the inn. He calmed his racing heart, and sniffed haughtily. Shame on her for giving him such a fright! He would go back to bed now, and maybe be tired enough to finally fall asleep.

"Young boy..." spoke a silvery voice, chiming bells echoing with each word, resonating every note.

Hercule whirled back around, unnerved. How dare she address him so casually! Fool woman, could she not see he was a vempar? A higher race than lowly goblins, and of noble rank?

"Do you know of the Swan?" The woman's voice chimed, as

she watched him through large, tilted eyes rimmed in pink eyelashes. Even the way she moved was unnerving, like a gliding ghost. "Have you seen a girl with eyes the shade of lilacs and hair the red of roses? Or perhaps," she asked further, "your ears have caught rumor of a Scourgeblood?" She hummed, bells chiming, swaying in thought. "I must find her...I must have the Swan."

Hercule had no idea what the woman was talking about, nor did he care.

'Swan? Scourgeblood? Her brain must be the size of a bean,' he scoffed in thought. He wanted to leave and get a good night's rest.

"Go wet yourself, you old hag," he grumbled. "Your idiotic questions are beneath one such as me." He raised his nose to the air, trying to look down on her despite his young height. "But here's a *real* question for you: Do you have any idea who I am? Hmm?" He sniffed. "Not only are vempars superior, but I'm the heir of House Dragonsbane. Don't ever address me so informally again. I should have you whipped!" He covered a yawn then. "I will, if you bother me tomorrow. But right now, I'm too tired. *Hmph*, lucky you."

He turned his back on the pond and the strange woman.

The breeze returned suddenly, swirling around the courtyard and growing fierce.

Hercule tried to shield his hair from getting whipped and messy as he ran for the door. No, he wanted to run, but suddenly found he couldn't—his feet were stuck, as if glued to the ground.

"Huh?" He tugged at his legs, but they wouldn't budge.

The wind shifted, whirling around him, and only him. Sparks and flashes of crimson lightning came and went in the wind circling him, a continuous static rhythm.

"Never in all my life has a person dared speak to me so. You vile, arrogant child." The silvery voice echoed beyond the rushing air. It was difficult to make out the cloaked figure through the spirals of crimson and hot sparks, the wind increasing in momentum. "You think that because of your race and rich heritage the world is handed to you on a silver platter? That everyone else is beneath you? Well…"

Tilted eyes glowed like fire beyond the swirling veil of wind that now encased him like a cage. His feet still wouldn't budge. How was that woman *doing* this?

Her laughter echoed like many chiming bells. "You say you are of Dragonsbane. So, of dragons I will make you!"

Electric sparks filled the air, streaking his vision. His mouth gaped wide and a strangled scream escaped his throat. Markings of strange words appeared from the sparks, and they seared into the skin of his left shoulder and breast, branding him like iron out a furnace. It burned, it *writhed*. Hercule tried to grab at his shoulder, but the pain was too intense to even touch.

"You say that your race is superior, above others," the voice continued in mirth, "So, above all others you will fly!" The chimes rang. "Three days of every full moon, and whenever your anger burns to rage, you will fear for your miserable life."

The markings across his shoulder and chest started to glow, becoming white hot embers, spreading beneath his skin and throughout his body. And then…his body changed.

Hercule held up his hands in horror as his fingers and nails lengthened, twisted, sharpened, grew into huge claws—the same thing happening to his feet and toes.

"*GroaH!*" he cried out.

Something shot out from the middle of his back, stretching upwards and towering over his head like tattered black cloth on hooks. No, the hooks were bone, and the material moved at his will, like bat wings. Another something sprouted out his lower back and tail bone: long and ridged, flexible as a whip.

Hercule tossed about frantically. He felt his head, the features of his perfect face stretching, distorting, elongating. Teeth growing, jaw jutting out. *"Gwoah— Roahhr!"* He couldn't recognize his own voice anymore as he screamed.

The woman laughed once more before vanishing in the sparks. "Learn the high price of your pride, young Dragonsbane. Farewell, or rather, fare-ill."

The changing of his body finally stopped, and Hercule collapsed on the grass, gasping for air, catching ragged breaths as his body shuddered all over.

The woman was gone. And sounds of people, having been wakened by his screams, came from the inn.

Hercule tried to sit up, but his legs weren't acting right. He frowned down at them, then stared wide-eyed at what he saw. He lurched over to the pond's edge, clumsily on all fours, and stared at the golden-eyed reflection looking back at him from the water. The eyes were the same as his own, but the rest of him…was the body of a dragon.

White opal scales glistened, reflecting colors of his surroundings. Black sails of bat skin rose for wings. Horns grew out from a scaly head with a narrow snout.

"Is there something out by the pond?" his sharp ears heard someone say.

'Oh no! They won't know it's me! The Draevs escorting us will kill me!' he thought.

Dragons were considered pests, eating livestock and attacking people who got in their way. They were hunted and chased out of inhabited lands, forced to retreat and dwell in secluded areas. Rarely did they venture into civilization, and when they did, it was either because the dragon was young and ignorant, or very old and powerful.

Hercule was too young; he had no way of defending himself from skilled Draevs. They wouldn't hesitate; there'd be no mercy. He had to escape!

The full moon seemed to laugh down at him. Three days, every full moon, he would become *this?*

His throat rumbled and he scrambled to reach the bamboo forest just beyond the pond. His awkward gallop didn't slow until the trees became thick around him. His big, yet child-sized dragon body bumped against every tree and obstacle.

What should he do? Three days was a long time; everyone would be searching for him. Even once he changed back into a vempar, how could he suddenly appear before them as if nothing had happened?

Hi Father, Mother. I'm back from disappearing for three days. Sorry about that. Mother would tear him to pieces for the worry he'd cause! And Father...the punishment he would give would be worse than a death sentence.

The more Hercule tried to think of a plan, a way out of this nightmare, the more weary he became. Until finally his limbs stopped and he sank beneath a sheltering willow. He'd sniffed and listened but found no trail or evidence of the woman who'd cursed him. If he couldn't find her...find someone who could help him...

He shut his reptilian eyes. If anyone ever found out about the heir of House Dragonsbane's curse, it would ruin the family name...and Father would never forgive him.

6

Morning came, slowly passing into afternoon, and then fading to evening as Hercule remained hidden within the willow's shelter. His only plan now: stay there until all three days were over and he transformed back.

Dusk melted into night, and Hercule woke forlornly from a nap. *'Three days feels like forever…'* his mind groaned. He had a strange feeling that something had woken him, some sound, but nothing appeared to be out there in the surrounding trees. His dragon vision saw clearly in the dark.

Kch-k!

Hercule's wilty bat-wing ears lifted at the noise. Then a flicker of movement caught his left eye: silent, graceful movement like that of a Draev.

The vempar warrior was coming towards him!

Whether the Draev knew Hercule was there or not, they'd soon find out when they bumped into his large body.

'If I move, they'll attack me. But if I don't move, they're still going to find and attack me.'

Hercule gritted his long teeth as the vempar approached. He would have to run as fast as he could before the Draev could lash out with their Ability. If only he could fly or use fire breath, but he was too young and new. And just slashing his claws wasn't much of a defense.

Hercule waited until the vempar was almost on top of him, then launched himself into a leap at the Draev.

"Wha!" The male Draev fell backwards, startled, and that was enough to give Hercule time to veer around and run like a speeding horse through the trees, all four legs galloping.

It wasn't long before the sounds of pursuit followed. Thrown *things* struck the ground and trees close to Hercule's body as he fled. The *things* resembled spears, seeking to pierce Hercule through, instead *thunking* into dirt and bark. That must be the Draev's Ability. Those spears looked sharp and thick enough to damage dragon scales—or at least a child dragon's scales, such as his.

'Run—run—run!' was all he could think.

Many boulders and rocks jutted up from the forest floor, adding to the difficult task of running at full-speed, and Hercule couldn't get used to his body's awkward movements on four legs, his floppy wings and tail dragging behind. Brush and branches snapped off and crunched as he clumsily ran. The forest growth was becoming too thick, too close together. He stumbled over an unseen rock, leaving an easy-to-follow trail of damage behind him.

'The Draev is catching up! At this rate, I'll—'

Light flashed. A spear whizzed past his left cheek, the point just grazing his scaly skin before arcing downward.

'I'm not going to make it!'

A sudden, sharp pain burned his left forearm, happening so fast he didn't see or feel the spear at first. Wincing, he steered around a pile of boulders, then spared a quick glance down at the injury: Blood was seeping down his hand—or clawed paw—from a gaping hole above the wrist. The spear earlier—it had pierced through-and-out his scales as it fell to the ground.

'My hand's going numb.' Fear shot through him, almost worse than the pain, and he couldn't help it as his pace slowed. The hand was useless. He tried to use it like a crutch anyway and let adrenaline drive him on.

"It's a dragon! Maybe it has the boy in its stomach," came a shout.

Icy fear stung needles inside his chest. The Draev must see his colleagues nearby and was now shouting for them to join in the hunt. Hercule couldn't...he was barely avoiding this *one* Draev's attacks... If more came, he was as good as dead.

"Help me!" Hercule cried out in one breath—there was nothing else he could do—his voice sounding more like a squawky roar than words. *'Lord God, I admit it! I've been selfish and haven't listened to You at all. But I'll change that! Don't let me die here, please! I'll change that. Please don't let me die—!'*

7

It was bright morning when Lord Dragonsbane readied to inspect the other silk facilities—and when Butler Lynk came to Hercule's room and found him missing.

Marigold had been the first to notice his empty bedroom, but figured he was taking a shower or eating early breakfast someplace. Now, she shrank against the wall as the lord and lady bombarded her with questions, grilling her about why she didn't mention him missing *sooner*.

"What an ungrateful and irresponsible wretch. We should leave you here in this foreign land to fend for yourself!" Lord Renald stormed off.

Marigold trembled beneath her false mask of calm.

Lynk remained close by, and made attempts to ease the furious parents' concern, suggesting they give the young lord more time to turn up. Meanwhile, groups of search teams continued to investigate. She wanted to give him a grateful hug; the butler had a way with words, able to soothe bad tempers.

As the day wore on, however, with no sight or sign of Hercule's whereabouts, the aristocrats reached the limit of their patience.

Lady Chatsalott was convinced he'd been taken captive by easterners. She moped and lay about the inn's bedroom chambers, kerchief in hand, her lady servant fanning her paling face with a giant feather fan. Chatsalott wailed and complained, a nonstop grating on the ears. "My poor little Hercule!" *Sniffle.* "Snatched away because of his family's high status. And now, here I am, wasting away in tears, unable to enjoy my vacation or even these delicious crumpets. So many more stores I wanted to visit...but how can I, in this distressed state of mine? *Bwoohoohoo*," she sobbed.

Lord Renald busied himself shouting at the search teams and the Draev squad leader, making their lives as miserable as he could. Meanwhile, Marigold did as Butler Lynk told her: "Stay out of sight and out of their minds. Don't draw any attention to yourself."

And so, Marigold twiddled her bare toes in the back courtyard pond, using a twig to maneuver a lotus closer, so she could sniff its pretty pink petals. It reminded her of the golden lotus from faeryn myth: said to exist somewhere in the deep of Magica Forest. The twig finally caught, and she pulled the flower up, sniffing in the sweet scent, then tying it in her hair above her long right ear.

Loud argument drifted from the paper windows of the inn's common room. Another Draev must have returned empty-handed, now getting scolded. Marigold got up and dashed toward the bamboo trees—the closest place to hide. The waxy green trunks of bamboo swayed, their narrow long leaves shimmering in the hot sunbeams, rustling and clacking together in a pleasant rhythm above her head. These woods…it brought back feelings of her forest home, though their sound was strikingly different. She missed wandering the forest floor, missed not remembering the images clearly.

Hm, why not use this opportunity and do some exploring? Wander the trees as she once loved to? For the first time since becoming a slave, Marigold giggled, the sun-filled air warm on her angel-cake skin as she melted away into the deep foreign woods…

Coming across a rock-strewn stream, with a boulder perfect for sitting above the babbling waters, Marigold took a seat, the sun shining down warming it.

She smoothed the skirt of her olive-green dress—not as constraining as some of the other dresses were. Personal slave attendants had to look presentable and refined, but the lace and ruffles were annoying. "I wish their hearts weren't made of stone," she said to no one in particular, resting chin on knees, and watching orange minnows swim against the current. "Is that what money does to people?"

The water gurgled. "No. The heart is already corrupt. Money simply reveals it."

She turned with a start at the low rumbling voice, a voice like that of a giant whispering, and the boulder underneath her quivered.

Twin large, sunburst orange discs appeared to either side as she sat there: a pair of eyes. But that meant, what she was sitting on was—

'A giant snout?' She almost rolled off into the stream.

Now that she could make out the head, she could see the rest of the body's outline, its scales blending in perfectly with the nature surroundings. No wonder she hadn't noticed the creature until now—a forest-dwelling dragon. An adult, judging by the long length. In stories, they were camouflaged predators, and only seen when they wished to be. Their scales able to mimic almost any background, changing color, shape, and even texture. *This* dragon's appearance was like boulders overgrown with moss and lichen, and a twisted tree trunk.

"Be still, two-legs child, you are far too thin for a meal."

She stared up at the orange orbs, one large eye at a time, and wrung her hands behind her. The dragon grumbled, the snout she stood on vibrating with the sound. "I only revealed myself because you appear distraught. Of all the races which litter this world, faeryn have been kinder to me."

Marigold felt her eyes and cheeks were wet. She rubbed them, not noticing the tears until now, ashamed.

The dragon rumbled, "…And also because yours are not the only tears being shed here."

What? She followed to where the big eyes looked, upstream, and she heard a soft moaning coming from *something* beyond. With a questioning look back at the dragon, she stepped off his nose onto the mossy ground. Then slowly, and curiously, she made her way up the rocky bank. Where the stream eventually leveled out into a small pool, the moaning came louder.

Hercule lay on his belly in the lukewarm water of a shallow pool, formed by a tranquil stream trickling through and filling the level area. His legs and arm he tucked underneath like a deer, black wings floppily folded against his back. The left arm he kept outstretched in front, blood seeping like red mist in the waters from the gaping wound. He tried licking it, but nothing would make it heal faster.

Could he Heal like a vempar in this form? At least he was alive, even though he was still amazed as to *how*. He remembered running, seeing a slope with a curved boulder jutting out its side like a shelter, then quickly ducking inside. There, he'd waited. But for some odd reason, the Draevs hadn't followed. Had something *else* caught their attention? It was too convenient for a mere coincidence. Lord God must have answered his plea, which meant Hercule would have to keep the promise he'd made in return.

The sound of a sharp gasp caught his ear, and he tilted his head to the grassy bank across the pond, heart thumping. What stood there at the water's edge startled him more than any Draev.

'*Marigold?!*'

The honey-blonde faeryn stood motionless, large mint eyes focused on the young dragon, black rag-like wings and smooth opal scales resting in the shallow water.

The moaning stopped when it noticed her, its golden gaze intense, so beautiful and mystical. Wonder lit Marigold's face before she gasped in horror at the wound and blood-tinted water. "How cruel! How could somebody do this? You poor creature."

Step after careful step, she waded near the injured dragon, not wanting to frighten it, and unsure if he was willing to let her get close.

Hercule started, instinct telling him to run, as she slowly approached. '*Calm down, she doesn't know it's me. The son of a nobleman must always remain calm in a crisis,*' he told himself.

Should he let her come close? There were no feelings of hate or fear coming from her, and it looked like she might plan on helping him, instead of calling for the Draevs. His mind churned, undecided, until she was already at his side and kneeling beside his injured arm. It was astonishing how quiet and smooth her unheard footsteps had been, the grace with which a faeryn moved through nature.

"There, there…" her voice soothed, examining how deep the wound was. "It's a hole, clean through. What *did* this?"

The dragon's reptilian gaze stayed on her intently. She was quite small compared to him, like a child to a pony.

'That gold color,' Marigold thought. *'I've seen golden eyes like that before…'*

Hercule, and his father. They had golden eyes, an inherited trait of the Dragonsbane bloodline. A fitting last name, indeed, the way their irises matched this dragon's so perfectly.

"Don't you worry, sir dragon, I'll help you. *Ehm*, I wish I had Healing power like vempars do." Her eyebrows drew down and she focused on the task of taking off the skirt slip from under her dress to use for a bandage, carefully wrapping it around the arm and temporarily stopping the bleeding.

Hercule watched, until a wave of weariness washed over him. *'I never would have expected the slave to come help me. Why is she helping me? If I'd seen a dragon, I would've had it hunted down, immediately—no matter if it was injured or not. Yet, she…she…'* A weary sigh escaped him, and inside he admitted she was a better person than him. Far better.

The many different shades of blonde in her hair glistened each time a ray of sunlight touched them. Liquid sunlight, to match a heart made of sunshine. Her hands felt soft and delicate while wrapping the fabric around him, soft as a butterfly's touch, her voice a lullaby in a comforting breeze.

A pang of regret struck his chest. He'd been so mean to her—hurt her, bossed her around, getting her into as much trouble as he could. Enjoying it, laughing. And yet, she was the one person here, now, tending to him when he needed help most. True, she didn't know it was Hercule she was helping, but he had the feeling that, even if she did know, she would still help. That was the kind of person she was— the kind of person *he* was supposed to be.

'How can she love others so easily? I hate people; they've always hated me and used me for my family name.' The frustration and anger it created inside him he took out on those beneath him.

And yet, she…

'I said things to her I never should have,' he thought with guilt.

"Hm?" Marigold was staring up at him. She reached a hand to his scaly opal face—he resisted the urge to flinch—and she wiped something from underneath his eye. "You're crying? You must be sad and scared…but don't worry, sir dragon. Your arm will heal up, and I know just the person to help!" Face alight with a plan, the girl bounded to her feet. "Wait here!" She sprinted away, barefoot.

How could the girl step along water, rocks, and fallen branches like it was all smooth carpeted floor on bare feet? *'Wait— Who is she planning to go get?'*

An hour later, the faeryn returned, with Butler Lynk in tow, pulling him along by the hand.

"I don't see what you're going on about, little maiden, but this…"

Lynk's sentence ended when he saw the dragon. Marigold tugged at him to keep moving. "He isn't dangerous! He's young, like me, I think. You can Heal him, can't you?" The girl's big pleading eyes and puckered lips begged.

With a groan and shake of the head, Lynk gave in, cautiously placing his hands on the injured arm and channeling repairing cells through his *essence*, Healing the damage from the inside out. The wound was soon gone, opal scales again smooth as a fish.

Lynk had to leave quickly or risk drawing suspicion from the lord and lady, should they call for him and find him gone. But Marigold chose to stay behind, for as long as she could, content just to sit there beside the dragon, her dress damp from the pond.

They watched the sun fall behind the trees together, and only then did she leave, for the same reasons as Lynk, but promised she'd be back in the morning.

It was surprisingly comforting, having her there, and when she left, Hercule felt a bit sad. She'd covered him up with wide tropical leaves, bush limbs and such first, to hide him, before whispering "Good night."

He wanted to beg her not to leave but could only rumble. She laughed, patting his snout.

Watching her go was painful, the little beam of sunshine. He didn't want to sleep in the forest alone again. The air held a chill, and mysterious calls of the night made his pulse jitter. The snort of a big black-and-white bear made him jump, though it lumbered away.

Only achy weariness forced his body to finally doze off.

When the first fingers of dawn stretched out, Marigold returned, with a basket in the crook of her arm full of bread, dumplings, and boiled eggs pinched from the breakfast table. He'd never seen a more beautiful sight.

8

Marigold grew more worried than ever about Hercule's whereabouts, as she watched the days pass and the distraught noble family pray each night when another search team returned empty-handed. At dawn on the fourth day, she made her way to the inn's back courtyard with a basket in hand, and suddenly, there sitting at the pond's edge, was Hercule.

His pearl-gray hair frizzed in a moppy mess, skin covered in scratch marks, and…no clothes. Instead, he had some sort of blanket wrapped around his waist and over his left shoulder.

"Hercule!" she exclaimed.

Others must have heard her cry, as footsteps came running.

A shriek of surprise, joy, then horror at Hercule's condition rang from Lady Chatsalott's lungs like an opera singer when she arrived. The poor woman fell into a faint, and her lady-in-waiting furiously fanned her face. Lord Renald came on her heels, saw the state of his son, and ordered Butler Lynk and Marigold to get Hercule cleaned up and dressed properly. He would speak to him afterwards.

Hercule managed to hide the markings on his skin from Marigold, who helped fix his hair and laid clean clothes out. But Butler Lynk clearly saw as he helped the nobleson wash and scrub clean. The black ink shapes stood out across his fair skin, but Lynk didn't say a word. Hercule hoped he would remain silent about it.

After he was made presentable, Father saw him and began a wave of questions: "What did the kidnappers look like? How did they capture you? Where did they take you, and how did you escape?"

Hercule's mouth hung open. *'They think I was… Good. Good! Let them believe that,'* he thought. He quickly fabricated a tale that it had happened in the dark of night by the pond, and someone threw a bag over his head. He never saw the kidnappers, or the place they held him, but the commotion of vempars out searching every inch of the city had made the captors nervous. Enough for them to give up and toss him into the woods, take the rope off his wrists and leave him in the dark without a stitch on but a blanket, where he then wandered until he recognized the bamboo woods and spotted the inn's tiered roof.

Everyone believed the story, or seemed to. A case of kidnappers realizing they'd bitten off more than they could chew could be credible. Hercule sighed in relief and was very grateful for the delicious hot soup and steamed buns served to him.

One full moon of the curse down. Now, the rest of his life left to go.

Marigold stood at the grassy pool where the young dragon had rested these past few days: He was gone, and she wondered if she would ever see him again. The days spent with the dragon had been the most fun she'd had in a long time. She would miss that.

Her left hand brushed over her heart.

vening, the day before the next full moon...
Hercule noted the calendar up on his bedroom wall.
Peering out the window, down onto Dragonsbane Mansion's front courtyard, he decided to sneak away before the curse activated.

He had wanted to stay in Higashi longer, hoping to somehow track down the goblin woman who'd cursed him, but Father had finished all his inspections.

He couldn't tell his family about his shameful curse, nor risk the consequences that would follow. He was the only heir of House Dragonsbane. He couldn't let his House's reputation fall to ruin because of him.

Even if he *had* stayed longer, Hercule had a feeling he wouldn't find the woman. She had vanished as easily as she had appeared that night.

"Three days..." How ironic it was. All the world's riches were in his grasp—he had everything and could get anything he wanted—yet his life felt as empty and pointless as the koi fish forever circling in the backyard pond. And now, when he truly *really* wanted something—freedom from the curse—it was impossible to purchase and as elusive as smoke.

Hercule peeked into the adjoining bathroom, where Marigold's pallet lay underneath a window. It was a spacious room, long and tiled, plenty of light, and a rug where she slept. It felt strange being around her now, ever since she'd befriended his dragon form. Not in a bad way, just...he wasn't sure how to behave around her anymore.

He regretted how cruel he'd been, the things he'd said... He shut his eyes a moment, remembering the promise he'd made Lord God that he would change his behavior. Now he had to learn how to be a better person and care about others—*sigh*, it wasn't going to be easy.

"I'm leaving early in the morning, before you wake up, to go and stay with my cousin," he said, as Marigold was arranging sheets on her little mattress of a bed. "As you heard me tell Father, I'll be away for three days or so, getting some piano lessons in and a change of scenery. You won't be coming with me. So...so do whatever you like when there isn't cleaning to be done!"

He shut the bathroom door, blocking her view of his room and his coloring cheeks. "I need my rest now, so keep out of my room until morning."

He could've said it more nicely, maybe, but if he behaved *too* nicely, she might grow suspicious. That was his excuse, anyway.

With a light backpack slung over a shoulder, Hercule climbed over his room's balcony and descended, clinging to the drainpipe, scaling down the wall.

He kept his cool, until both his feet touched firm ground.

'Yes. I made it!'

"Leaving at this late hour, milord?"

Hercule froze, then slowly faced the speaker. Head Butler Lynk had been passing by the wall.

"I…" Hercule searched for excuses, "I decided to leave now, instead of waiting for morning."

"Oh? I'll fetch the carriage for you right away, milord."

"No! I'll…do it myself."

The man's blond eyebrows rose, and Hercule tried not to seem nervous. "You're a servant, remember? Your job is to obey Dragonsbane, and that's what I am: a Dragonsbane. I already have the carriage waiting for me, so leave me alone." Sweat beaded his temples. "Father knows, so don't go bothering him about it. And, and…don't say any more on the subject, butler."

Hercule marched away, not waiting to see what the man would do. He couldn't scare him properly into keeping quiet, since Lynk was a paid servant of Father's. He could only hope.

The servants' door clicked as Lynk must have gone indoors. It bothered him why Lynk hadn't asked about the strange markings on his body. He was sure Lynk had seen them—scrubbing the dirt off his back, how could he not? But why stay silent about it?

Rounding a corner, Hercule made a dash for the backyard field and the stretching woods beyond—the woods which eventually joined into Cherryblossom Park's secluded forest. He would find a good hiding place there. It might be safer to get out of the city altogether, but that thought scared him more. He didn't want to be alone outside the city walls where anything might roam.

He trotted off across the twilight lit field, the moon rising above.

All morning and noon Marigold spent doing chores. The hateful housekeeper ran her ragged washing curtains, sheets and tablecloths which already looked perfectly clean. Then she helped in the kitchen with lunch. Before the grumpy maid could find more work for her to do, Butler Lynk distracted her, giving Marigold a chance to escape. She left the bustling world of the mansion, dashing outdoors to the backyard.

The sky was rich blue, the sun bright and warm. Marigold kicked off her black maid shoes and ran barefoot through the lush grass. Beyond the pond, a copse of trees melted into woods—woods which beckoned her to be explored.

Hercule sat on his rump, once again in the body of a dragon. This time he'd taken off all his clothes and placed them in the backpack, which he then hid under some bushes for later. He'd brought food: ten loaves of bread, which right now didn't feel like much.

But there was one thing he didn't prepare for: how bored he would be for three days straight.

'I should be used to this. I've always been alone.' He glowered at himself.

A movement to his left made him jump. His limbs crouched, ready to run. When the small source of commotion appeared, he almost fell on his dragon face.

'Marigold? I can't believe this girl found me again!'
Marigold looked equally as startled, then her mouth broke into a thrilled grin. "Fireye, you're here!" She hopped up, small arms embracing his long neck in a hug, standing on tippy toes to reach.

Hercule wasn't sure how to respond—no one ever really hugged him, and he preferred it that way. He raised a clawed hand and gave a sort of pat on her back. She giggled, so it must've been the right thing to do.

"I can't believe you're here! Did you follow me?" Her face beamed, then dimmed. "*Ehm*, this isn't a very safe place for you to live, though."

Hercule shook his head, agreeing.

"It's okay to visit, but you shouldn't stay long. Maybe the Outer Woods would be safer? No, I'm not allowed outside the city walls by myself," Marigold remembered.

Hercule rolled his eyes and nudged her shoulder with his snout.

She stumbled. "What, are you saying you can avoid getting caught here? *Hee*, a bit arrogant, aren't you?"

He glared.

"It's best not to take chances, Fireye. I mean, you don't want to end up caught, like I was."

Hercule's glare melted into guilt.

"But you are smallish, so…maybe it'll work for now?" She cocked her head, studying him. "You should practice using your camouflage. You know, blend into the scenery?"

He rumbled, and tried to imagine his scales changing color.

"*Nonono*, a darker green," said Marigold, observing. "Now make your arm look mossy."

Hercule tried, but his scales didn't listen like they should, and he soon gave up, flopping his head and long neck to the dirt with a grunt. He felt her climb up on his back and sit there. He raised his head to glare at her, but she didn't notice, swinging her legs back and forth.

"Do you ever get lonely?" she asked suddenly.

He thought. '*Yes. Too often.*'

"I wonder if that's how Hercule feels? Maybe that's why he

has an attitude," Marigold pondered. "He's been acting different lately, though."

The dragon swallowed nervously.

"I used to feel empty, like him," she continued, gazing up at the canopy of leaves and dappled sunlight, "before I was close to Father Creator." She shook her head. "I miss having friends, and Nonna and Papa... But I think that's a different kind of lonely."

Hercule glanced back at her, and she gave a mellow smile. He thought it over. It made sense that the Creator could give meaning and love to His creation, filling the emptiness, just like Hercule gave meaning to the music he played.

He rested his head on his back—which was an odd thing to be able to do—beside Marigold, and they watched the sunbeams play through the trees.

10

Early morning, Hercule washed his human face. Dabbing a towel around his cheeks, he noticed through the window Marigold: her small figure sneaking off into the woods, no doubt checking to see if the opal dragon was still there. If only he could tell her not to bother looking until the next full moon shone...

He managed to keep his relationship with Marigold kind yet distant, like an acquaintance, without raising suspicion. But as a dragon, he couldn't stop their friendship from growing. He'd become dear to her, the only friend in a world so different from her forest homeland. He wouldn't admit it out loud, but having her around made life better for him too, like a warm sunray piercing through the rain.

Every day now he practiced the piano, forcing his skills to improve since his monthly three-day "absences" were supposed to be him learning piano from his distant cousin. Playing the white and black keys over and over grew boring, so next he pretended his cousin was learning the violin, too, and would teach him that. The violin was a nice diversion, and in many ways suited him better.

After breakfast, Mother sought him out, looking eager about something. He frowned and prepared for the worst.

"Daaarling, I was just thinking, while getting my hair trimmed today, that you could use a little change." Mother's fingers brushed at his bangs. "Trim this back a bit, fluff the top up, yes?" she thought aloud, fiddling with his hair. "We could start a new hair trend among the young lords."

Hercule gazed up at Mother's hair: today styled as a wild, giant bow.

"My hair's fine the way it is. I don't need a change," he said.

"Oh, but it'd be such fun! And so cute. How do you feel about braids?"

"No."

"Just a little poof at the top? And add in some feathers?"

"No."

"I think it'd be—"

He wanted to slap her hand away but pushed it instead. "I said, no."

Trails of steam curled through the air, and she looked about. "My, is there a boiling teakettle somewhere? Where is this coming from?"

Hercule saw his reflection in a hanging ornamental silver platter on the wall, steam lightly swirling from his ears—it was coming from *him*.

The anger…his body wanted to transform into a dragon. Here. Now.

Panic lanced through him, replacing the anger, and with it the urge to transform faded.

Now he knew: if he grew angry enough, his body would transform on its own, and he couldn't control it but to calm his emotions.

In the end, he agreed to a hair trim in the back and some poof at the top to appease Mother. She took some gel and swirled the top of his head into a bird's nest before he could stop her, and looked quite pleased with herself.

"Milord." Butler Lynk met up with Hercule afterwards, careful to keep his lips from twitching up. "May I share some advice about dealing with—shall we say—difficult situations?"

Hercule's moody glare turned to him. "Fine."

Lynk coughed to keep from grinning. "Anger is like a living thing. It must be kept from growing the moment it is born. Let me give you an example: Anger grows like a flame. If you let your thoughts feed it, it will grow until every part of you burns. But if you stomp on it while it's still yet a tiny flame, cut off the thoughts and fill it with love, then it will die."

Hercule stared blankly at him.

"Give it a try, sometime. Just think in your head: *Stomp out the flame.*" He gave a wink and left.

'*If I thought he was strange before, I know he is now. Ah, that's right, I'm supposed to be kinder to people,*' Hercule reminded himself, slapping his cheek.

Despite his doubts, Hercule gave it a try when anger boiled in his gut again, stomping out the flame in his mind, replacing it with a simple, happy thought—a memory of dappled sunlight in calm woods, with Marigold on his back.

Surprisingly it helped, and the steam from his ears and mouth dissipated.

Years passed, and once again a lavish birthday party was being held: for Hercule's twelfth birthday, in the heat of May. The fancily dressed guests came, and expensive gifts made a tower upon one of the tables. Fake smiles and compliments were handed out as quickly as a virus, the same as always. And once again, he was glad when the day finally came to an end.

'I'm still a fish trapped in a pond,' he thought to himself.

"Ehm…milord?"

Hercule turned at the light, airy voice as he was about to head upstairs for the night. Marigold stood there, shuffling her feet bound in fancy shoes. There was a peculiar pink color to her cheeks. Butler Lynk was also present, behind her.

"Yes?" Hercule tried not to sound as weary as he felt.

"Um…I…" She was holding something behind her back. Lynk urged her on. "Mr. Lynk helped me make this for your birthday. I know it isn't much," she added hastily, "But…"

She stopped talking and held out to him a hand-woven, oval pillow: the outside soft velvet, inside stuffed with downy feathers. The front was an embroidered depiction of a golden lotus—big and beautiful—standing within a dark pond. A single object of beauty thriving in a dark place. "Mr. Lynk helped me find the materials and, *uhm*, guided me with the threading. I'm not very good at that sort of thing on my own…"

Hercule held the small, decorative pillow in his hands. *'She made this for me? Someone used their time to make something for me?'*

The pillow was beautiful. The most beautiful gift he had ever received. Love filled each stitch and thread.

"There's a meaning, too." Lynk urged her to continue, and she did, after a swallow.

"The flower is known as the *D'ore Lotus*, or Golden Lotus, said to grow in the darkest of places. It's a flower of myth and legend among forest faeryn, so rare that there are no recorded sightings of its existence except through story." Her gaze flicked up to his, then back down, her cheeks coloring more. "*The one who is noble stands steadfast against the darkness*—that is the meaning of *D'ore Lotus*. Not noble as in wealth or status, but a person who is honorable, just, kind, and has understanding."

She glanced up at him once more, as if worried the gift might be a silly idea. With a jolt, he realized he'd been staring at her and saying nothing.

"Oh, ah..." His heart thumped, his mouth lost for words. The pillow's feather body sunk between his fingers. "This is beautiful," he said. She looked back up at him, doubtful. "It is! I mean it." He forced something he hoped was a smile on his face; he really wasn't good at happy facial expressions. "No one has ever given me such a special gift. You made this by hand? You must have a hidden talent."

A pleased smile filled her face.

Good; he'd used the right words. But this swirl of emotions was making him feel open and vulnerable. He shuddered.

Lynk's gaze shifted from Hercule to Marigold, then back to Hercule. "You're growing older. Perhaps it's time the little miss had her own room, not so close in vicinity to yours."

A furious blush reddened Hercule's countenance, and he berated the butler. "Lynk—! How could you—*that's*—I would never—!"

Lynk covered his grin with a gloved hand.

Hercule's red face steamed.

Lynk waved apologetically. "Apologies, apologies, milord. Don't forget the anger calming technique."

"There's something other than a flame I want to stomp out," Hercule muttered under his breath.

He exhaled, and a flash of light spilled from his breath.

He paused at the strange flash.

They both stared wide-eyed at him.

"Did I just…?" Hercule began, slack-jawed.

Lynk nodded. "Seems you've inherited your father's Ability with fire, milord. Though it's the first time I've seen fire spring from someone's *mouth*."

Hercule frowned behind his hand pressed to his lips. Did Lynk know more than he let on?

He had to wonder. But then, did he really want to know if he *did*? If Lynk was keeping quiet about the curse markings and Hercule's strange behavior, then he should simply be grateful and not ask questions.

11

One morning, Draev Master Nephryte appeared at the Dragonsbane Mansion's front doorstep. Both the housekeeper and head butler welcomed him in as an honored guest.

Lady Chatsalott was first to greet the Draev Master, hurrying faster than she ever had before for anything. The moment her eager eyes locked onto Nephryte's handsome features, the man sensed he was in trouble.

"Oo-hoohoohoo," she giggled, fanning a red feathered fan. Long eyelashes fluttered at him. "What an hooonor it is to have you visit, Master…Nephryte, was it? Such a charming name, fit for such a charming-looking young man." She chortled, covering her lips with the fan, and winking.

She held out her hand for him to kiss. He stared at it for a moment, stomach roiling, before he finally—light and brief—kissed her hand.

She giggled and swooned, fanning the fan outrageously. "Oo-hoohoo, Master Nephryte, such a naughty thing!" she tittered. "I should give you a spanking, young man."

Nephryte's mouth was a speechless line. The lady took a step forward and reached as if to touch his arm.

"Is that a bit of dust I spy on those rrrobust, muscular shoulders?" she rolled her R's fancily.

Nephryte gracefully dodged aside. "I'm here to see His Grace. To speak about his son's future," he tried to say, though the woman didn't seem to acknowledge a word of it.

Lord Renald appeared, thankfully, rescuing Nephryte before he was forced to flee. The lady subdued herself and pretended to be bored, waving the fan idly.

"Master Nephryte, welcome! Let us speak in my private study." Lord Renald nodded to his wife. "My dear, your hair is out of place. I would expect you to look more presentable for a guest."

The lady gasped in fright, feeling at her prong-shaped hairstyle.

The arrival of a powerful Draev Master would raise talk among Upper-town folk and earn Dragonsbane points over other relatives and Houses. Lord Renald seemed quite pleased.

Master Nephryte remained tense as a spring throughout the following meeting. The lady wouldn't stop secretly flirting and batting those long eyelashes, and the lord was just as much trouble with all his bragging and boasting!

Nephryte released an exhausted breath once he finally exited the mansion hours later. He used the excuse of wanting to meet Hercule and quickly left the room, following a servant who pointed out where the boy was.

The backyard pond was a peaceful sight, and the gardens and spreading field beyond even more so. He shuddered, never happier to leave a house in his life. "I don't think I can handle coming back here," he muttered.

He spotted the boy: pearl-gray hair brushed by the breeze, eyes more golden and fiery than his father's. The boy stood up from the pond's edge, coming toward him. There was an air of nobility in the way he carried himself, head held high, for someone so young.

"I understand your feelings. It's not the first time a man has refused to visit us again," Hercule commented frankly.

Nephryte couldn't help but chuckle, raising a hand to shield from the sun. "I can believe that."

"I assume you are here to evaluate my Ability. Are you to be my Draevensett Master?"

Nephryte blinked at his straightforwardness. "That's correct, Hercule." He smiled warmly and leaned forward. "My students are like family, so we'll have to get along well."

No emotion showed on Hercule's face. If anything, the boy looked bored. Perhaps he saw this as just another duty he must perform for the Dragonsbane name, and nothing more.

'Poor kid. Even though he has a blood-related family, in many ways he's alone, and carrying a mountain of responsibility,' thought Nephryte. He straightened. "I hear it was your birthday yesterday."

The boy almost rolled his eyes. Nephryte figured he might be tired of the celebrations and extravagant gifts he didn't really want.

"So, I brought something for you. Consider it a welcome gift for becoming my student. It's beside the carriage. I took it for a test run on my way here."

The boy lifted his face, interest now creasing his brow. Nephryte pulled out a pair of riding goggles, looping them over the boy's head. "Practice it around the yard until your head grows into these."

Hercule brushed at his hair, miffed, but anticipation got the better of him. "Well, I… I suppose I could have a look at it."

The Draev Master nodded, and then the wind picked up and the man seemed to glide up into the air as Hercule watched. He waved once, before soaring off on the wind.

Hercule watched in awe for a long moment, then tried not to run over to the carriage garage.

Once there, he scanned about. His mouth hung open at what was parked there against the garage's wall. Jet black, with sleek bladed fans for hovering: a bladecycle.

His prim parents would disapprove. Hercule grinned. Maybe Master Nephryte would be someone he could get along with well.

He adjusted the goggles around his face and hopped onto the black seat. The fans rumbled awake, spinning, lifting the contraption a foot off the ground. "I think I'll name it…Eclipse," he said.

The bladecycle glided fast over the mansion's acres of land, leaving blown grass trails in his wake.

A part of him feared going to Draevensett, how he would keep the curse a secret. With classes and student dorms, it was going to be much harder to escape when he needed to.

'I need to master my dragon scales' camouflage,' he thought with determination.

But fears aside, he wanted to master the power of fire and become his own person—not just be the heir of Dragonsbane. And Draevensett Academy may be the only way to achieve that.

One of the fish broke the surface of the pond as he rode past—leaping out over the grass towards a small rivulet and flowing freedom.

Twin Ravens' Flight

1

The rain began. Slowly at first, then it grew into a torrential downpour.

"Please be okay, please be okay..." the raven-haired boy whispered.

He brushed damp curly bangs from his forehead, his leather boots splashing in gathered pools along the uneven cobblestone street as he ran, ignoring the sheltering overhangs of shops.

Sheets of rain rippled as a gust of warm air passed through. Oilpowder streetlamps flickered on as dark clouds obscured the afternoon, as if it were night. Zarren turned at a lamp post, veering down a narrow side street. He was almost there.

"Please be okay..."

There it was! He reached the small stone house and tried to

catch his panting breath. It was a weathered, old house: off-white plaster peeling, stained over the years by colorful molds, wooden window frames chipped, a single dim lantern stuck above the front door. And it stood sandwiched between the bare walls of two shops, which both faced the well-traveled streets on either side. The house, however, faced the cramped, dirty alley, as if it wanted to hide.

Zarren quietly hurried through the door, his soaked hair dripping its own little rainstorm. He paused to listen.

There were the usual clicks of knitting needles: That would be Mother. So, she was okay.

He took off his drenched coat and boots, leaving them beside the door in the small entrance space.

"Zarren…" spoke a quiet voice.

He turned, relief replacing all the worry on his face, as another young boy of raven hair came down the rough, uneven staircase across from the entrance.

"Elijob." Zarren rushed forward, wrapping his arms tightly around his twin brother.

Elijob hugged back, patting his back. "I'm okay, nothing happened. You shouldn't worry so much every time we're apart. It was only thirty minutes you were gone."

'True,' Zarren thought. *'But anything can happen in even a single minute.'*

"Is he…here?" Zarren asked in a whisper.

Elijob shook his head. His hair was straighter, and trimmed shorter above the shoulders, but otherwise they looked almost identical, down to the same small elk-like antlers. But Elijob's features held a cheerfulness that Zarren could never match, a winning smile that could brighten the shadows.

"Did you find it?"

Zarren nodded and slipped the book out from underneath his jacket. The worn cover bore an illustration of three men dressed in blue, their swords raised to the sun. "A house seller was getting rid of it," he said.

"It's magnificent!" Elijob took the book as if it were a precious jewel, and not a poorly cared for antique. He flipped through the pages and colorful illustrations. "That seller had no idea what they were giving away! This is the best *Three Bladeers* copy we've ever come across. There's even a group of special edition stories included!"

Zarren's mouth lifted at the edges. "Now we just need to find a pair of rapiers to practice with."

"And the cool hats! We can't become cool swordsmasters without cool hats. It's a thing, you know."

Zarren chuckled at his twin's enthusiasm.

Becoming swordsmasters had been his and Elijob's dream since they first saw a *Three Bladeers* play being performed in the town square.

The danger, the swords, the camaraderie of the heroes, and the rescuing of those in need, drew Zarren in and filled his heart with adventure. He wanted that life—they both did. And becoming a master of the swords would offer that life.

Zarren glanced about. "We shouldn't be standing here in the open. Let's go read this upstairs," he said quietly.

The twins hurried up. They had barely reached the top step of the staircase when the entrance door opened, and stomping boots came inside. Recognizing the heavy gait, they didn't need to look to know it was *him*.

Zarren felt Elijob's hand grip his arm.

"Karen, I thought I told you to keep these floors clean! There's a flood of rainwater here," his hateful, gravelly voice blared.

Karen, their mother, quickly put away her knitting and hurried over with a cloth to scrub the floor. He grimaced, the rough hairs around his unshaven mouth and cheekbones grizzly.

The man didn't bother pointing out where the water was or acknowledging that he'd caused some of it himself, but stomped into the kitchen where he tossed his work-sack—brimming with blacksmithing projects to finish at home—messily on a chair. He would expect her to clean that up too, right away.

He scratched the base of his chipped rehfabel antlers, and his scowling face scanned the kitchen table and pitiful counters. "Where's the food?" he growled. "Dinner's supposed to be on the table!"

Mother's haggard features winced, shoulders tensing as she scrubbed vigorously at the floor. "It was—" she began. But he didn't let her finish.

"Where's the food, you lazy vempar?" He started cursing, and Zarren tried to cover his brother's ears.

Mother rose to stand, but not fast enough before he crossed the room and grabbed her braided black hair, yanking it hard so that she yelped. "It's…in the fridge…" she strained to speak against the pain. "It's ready! I…*ngh*…only have to take it out."

He gripped the braid a moment longer, then finally released her. "Then get it out, you worthless wench." He muttered the last under his breath as she scurried to the fridge. "Why do I put up with a lazy, ugly mule? Worthless, worthless; never knew a tramp so worthless…"

Plates clattered as Karen shakily set the pre-fixed meal of fish and lettuce out on the table. She hid her trembling hands in her apron, knowing that seeing her fear would only make him all the angrier.

Slouching hard onto one of the creaky old chairs, the man's lips curled in disgust at the plate, even though he grabbed the fork and began eating anyway. "This dung heap again?" He made a bitter sound. "There'd better be something with real flavor tomorrow." He chomped and swallowed.

While he ate, Mother quickly went back to scrubbing the

hallway floor dry. Zarren and Elijob used the distraction to continue from the top step and into their shared bedroom.

"We should leave, run away," said Zarren, his throat tight with emotion. His fingers clenched the sill of the small window in their low-ceiling room.

"We can't abandon Mother..." Elijob's voice sounded equally pained. He neared the window to stand at his brother's side, facing the view just as Zarren turned to face away from it. "Besides, *he* would find us. You know he would find us. *That man...is relentless.*" Elijob swallowed.

Zarren shut his eyes, front teeth biting his lip. Elijob spoke true. They would be running for their lives, forever, until he found them.

At times, Zarren found himself hating Mother for getting pregnant out of wedlock by such a wicked person. Carrying twins, and with no place to go, she'd felt there was no other choice but to live with the father and serve him like a slave. She said it was better than the alternative of a brothel house, and so wouldn't listen to any suggestions about running away.

"Every boy needs a father," she'd say. But they would have been far better off never knowing him at all.

Elijob slipped the old book under their bed for safekeeping.

Thmp, thmp!

Heavy footsteps began coming up the staircase. Zarren moved to stand in front of Elijob, but his twin gently pushed him aside. "No, Zarren. It's my turn."

"Elijob..." Zarren wanted to protest, but his kindly brother insisted it was only fair that they take turns. One person couldn't bear all of it alone.

The door slammed open, and the unshaven man entered. "Let's see here. Which one of you deserves punishing today?" he said, like a predator calculating its next meal. The twins shuffled back a step, unable to suppress their fear. They could smell the alcohol thick on him.

Elijob readied himself and faked a sneeze—an annoying sound that would bring rage down upon him.

"You piece of dog dung!" The man grabbed Elijob's arm, squeezing, and began dragging him out the door. "How many times have I said: Keep your *disgusting* coughing and sneezing to yourself, huh?"

It was all Zarren could do not to rush after Elijob and rescue him. But he couldn't, he knew he couldn't. Tomorrow would be his turn.

"Let's see what we can do to shut your sneezing up," the man slurred drunkenly.

Elijob didn't struggle but flashed one last smile to his twin as he was dragged down the staircase.

Zarren couldn't restrain a gasp of protest, his feet moving after them.

"What's this, are you feeling left out?" The man boomed a laugh over his shoulder. "I'll be coming for you soon, don't worry. Nothing better to do on a miserable day like this."

Zarren saw Elijob's pained expression, wishing his twin had kept quiet and let things be.

Zarren stood rigid on the top step, watching until Elijob and the man turned to exit the back of the house, where a tiny herb garden and the off-kilter tool shack was. The backyard door opened and slammed shut.

Zarren fell to his knees, legs collapsing underneath him. *'I wish…I wish…'* he thought, and tears blurred his vision. Soon, his twin's stifled yelps could be heard, and Zarren clenched the sides of his head, trying to shut it all out.

He hummed a calming tune to himself.

Teardrops pattered the wood stairs. He and Elijob had more vempar blood in their veins, unlike *that man*, and so their wounds Healed without a trace. The memories, the emotional pain, however, would never Heal.

Living in a small fishing town, in the Draeth Kingdom of vempars, their next-door neighbors didn't care much when they heard the boys' cries of pain. It would all Heal up just fine, they assumed.

But vempars were not immortal. If their body was injured repeatedly, faster than it had time to Heal, they could die just like any other humanoid race.

"Elijob…"

It felt like an eternity before Zarren heard the heavy footsteps re-enter the house. His turn had come.

He numbed his mind to it. Numbed as he was dragged by his curly hair through the pouring rain outside, into the backyard and thrown against the muddy ground so hard that stars danced in his vision. The rain pattered in ever-growing puddles around him.

"Every day, it's always the same," the man said with drunken bitterness. "I go off to forge in the manufacturing facility, and every day somebody points out my antlers and gives me crap about it. Every day somebody reminds me I'm just a half-vempar whose mother got pregnant far from home with some disgusting rehfabel, before she ran back to her kind. Do you know what it's like? *Do* you? No, your antlers are so small, so easy to hide." The man slapped Zarren's head. "And you can Heal, unlike me. You've got more vempar blood in you, thanks to your worthless mom. You just fit right in." The man lifted something from the ground. "I hate that."

Zarren felt a metallic object strike his legs, then hit across his ribs. He numbed himself to the pain, and soon Zarren began to lose consciousness. He didn't fight but let the world and its sounds fade into darkness.

2

Blue-winter eyes opened a fraction, then slowly focused, as Zarren regained consciousness.

The cloud-covered dusk was high overhead, and soft raindrops fell calmly about him as he lay motionless on the slick ground. How long had he lain there?

He dreaded the thought of moving; his body felt numb but would come alive with pain as soon as he did. After several breaths, he dared to move his arms. The Healing had been at work, but sharp pains still lanced through his limbs, and a gash on his face burned.

"Elijob?" Zarren coughed, wiping blood away with a sleeve; he forced himself to sit up and shift his shirt back down. His neck carefully turned until he spotted the shack and limped toward it. Peering through the gloom and rising mist, he found his twin sprawled on his side, unmoving.

"Elijob!" Zarren dropped to his knees and wrapped both arms around his twin. He helped him roll over, cupping the back of the boy's head in his hand. His other hand brushed hair away from Elijob's face. Angry tears streaked down his cheeks. Welts were still Healing on his brother, and his broken left hand slowly repaired. Clenching his jaw until it hurt, Zarren pulled a splinter from Elijob's shoulder.

Elijob blinked awake, gazing up into his twin's pale, worried face. "You…okay?"

Zarren shook his head, rain mixing with tears. "I'm always fine." He hugged Elijob's weak body to his chest, cradling his head against him. He didn't deserve this. Kind Elijob, who would never hurt anyone. He didn't deserve this!

Rage boiled inside Zarren. The rain pelted them steadily through the night, and he ignored it, sitting in the muddy sludge.

In the first touches of dawn, the twins quietly left the house and went on their way to the town's lakeshore, with small nets to catch fish in hand. It was their summer chore and routine, since buying meat in town was expensive and *that man* refused to help pay for any. This morning, the street they took was busier than usual. A loud voice was speaking out, and some people had gathered to listen.

Elijob paused at the edge of the crowd, trying to see between people. Zarren hesitated but joined him.

"The world is tainted in darkness. It has been ever since the day Adam, the first human, disobeyed Lord God and brought sin into his heart and into us, his descendants." The man who spoke was tall, and not just because of the crate he stood on.

His brown hair tossed about in the breeze cutting through town, and his eyes, a piercing blue, seemed to see straight through his soul. Zarren quickly ducked his head away.

"But there is still hope. Our Creator did not abandon us to our fate, but sent His Son to wash away our sins with His blood, so that when we die, we will live with Him in His kingdom in Heaven, until the future day when He will remake all of the worlds anew," declared the man. Some in the crowd grumbled, a few laughed and left, but the man wasn't deterred. "Lord God is our hope! He is the solid rock we can hold on to, even through the fiercest of storms. The hope He gives is true, and His promises never fail to those who love and follow Him."

Zarren began to walk away.

"He is your salvation, if you put your trust in Him and believe in what He did."

Salvation…hope…if only there was such a thing. He and his brother could sure use that.

Zarren continued away, and Elijob trotted to catch up.

At a worn, abandoned dock they fished for hours, and by late morning had caught nothing but a single red herring.

Zarren took the punishment of another beating, *that man* ranting about having a worthless son who couldn't fish. Mother begged him to stop, but that only earned her a fist to the cheek.

Zarren had to shut Elijob inside the kitchen closet to keep his twin from trying to take his place. Zarren held a shaky breath, numbing his mind once again as he vaguely felt himself being pulled towards the shack.

Hours later, he heard himself whimpering. "I can't take this anymore."

Elijob rubbed a comforting hand along Zarren's back as he sat slumped on his knees before the window in their shared room. His whole body quivered as it worked to Heal itself.

"I can't anymore," Zarren whispered at the floor, his tears

long since used up.

Elijob closed his eyes, heart aching for his suffering twin. After a hushed moment, he finally spoke. "Okay," he said, then again more firmly, "Okay! Let's go. Let's get out of this horrible life—run away, like you said before." He kissed Zarren's forehead, wrapping both arms around his twin's shoulders as they shook.

What would he do without such a dear brother, thought Zarren. He never would've been able to last this long, if not for him. He was his support, his best friend, his whole life. The one who understood him most.

"R-remember this morning?" Elijob said, attempting to keep his own voice from sobbing. "That tall person said Lord God is our hope and rock, even through the fiercest storm, if we trust Him. Well," he sniffled, "I think we need to trust Him now, cry out to Him."

"You really believe all that?" asked Zarren.

Elijob nodded. "I do." He clasped his twin's hand in his and prayed, asking for God's salvation and freedom. Then he nodded to his twin, "Let's run away."

Zarren gripped his hand in return. "In the morning, after *he* leaves for work, we'll make our escape."

The pale fingers of dawn stretched to push back the night through a gray sheet of rainclouds. *That man* made his way out the front door, work-sack slung over a shoulder, stomping off down the alley to the connecting main street up ahead. Now was their chance!

Zarren and Elijob hurried downstairs, already prepared with a backpack stuffed of bread, clothing and supplies, and their treasured book. They wore matching dark trousers and suspenders, white shirtsleeves and frayed jackets.

Mother was in the kitchen, busy cleaning.

"Mother!" Elijob rushed to her. "Come away with us. We don't have to live like this anymore. We'll find a better place, a *better* way."

Her features, at first shocked, softened into a quiet sadness as she understood. "Running away…? I can't. I can't go with you."

"But *why*? Just come with us!" Elijob pleaded.

Her fingers trembled on the table. "It's better to stay on his good side," she whispered.

Zarren stomped his foot. "No, it's a living nightmare, and you know it! Getting away from *this* is worth anything. Stop being afraid, and come!"

She gave them a partial smile, and brushed back his bangs with a shaky hand, palm cupping his cheek. "I have to stay…but you don't. Go, find a new life, and think of me."

Zarren bit his lip, making it bleed, and shook his head. "He'll take it out on you once he learns we've gone!"

"True," Mother said, and pulled out a leather fold from a drawer. "I will leave soon, but not with you. Perhaps we can meet up in the capital city, in a few days. Here." She placed the leather in Zarren's hand. "You'll need this to pay the entrance fee. Once you're there, go to the center of the city where the Draev Guardian Headquarters is."

"Why there?"

"It's a safe place for those in need," she said simply, and got out the knife for peeling carrots. Her head lowered, long black hair spilling forward to shadow her face. "Go. You'll need as long of a head-start as you can get."

Zarren had doubts, but it was true they needed a long head-start. "Promise you'll meet up with us?"

"I promise." She gave them each a quick hug, then turned her back as she chopped the carrots.

Zarren glanced backward one last time, memorizing Mother's features, before stepping out the door.

Elijob grasped Zarren's hand, holding it tight to offer his twin courage, as well as to give himself some, and their journey began down the cobbled main street. With this head-start, they should reach the city by evening, following the road south.

They were *really* doing this. Fear and excitement of the unknown raced through Zarren. He glanced sidelong and saw the same thrill and hope on Elijob's face.

The town came to an end at the low, shabby stone wall which encircled it. The cobblestone street became a dirt path as it continued through the old arched gateway. The gatekeeper on a creaky chair eyed them curiously but didn't speak as they passed—ignoring anybody who was leaving the town.

Outside the lichen-ridden wall, they could see Lake Doroth to their right, its overcast waters lapping at the shore and dingy docks. They waved farewell in unison to the great lake and turned their backs, heading south down the dirt road, which stretched onward through open fields.

The land became thick with wide varieties of grasses and wildflowers, and woods spread off to their right.

"Look, Brother!" Elijob's hand pointed to the sky ahead. "The merry sun has come out to greet us." With a playful laugh, he charged ahead.

Zarren couldn't help but smile. Narrow rays of sunlight pierced through the somber clouds, and bits of it touched down upon Elijob's raven hair and pale face, like a promising ray of hope. His twin skipped about, carefree and arms spread wide.

Zarren shook his head and shoved his twin playfully with an elbow. "You say the strangest things, like some odd poet. What makes you think the sun is merry?"

Elijob giggled, shoving back. "Because it smiles down on us," he said as if it was obvious.

"That's a made-up expression people use—the sun can't actually smile." Zarren laughed.

More rays of light blossomed through the clouds, and a semi-cool breeze rose to ruffle their bangs. Wildflowers of sunburst orange, yellow, white, magenta and lilac carpeted the landscape like a wild garden. Elijob picked one of each kind, and some black-eye sunflowers and purple heather, creating a bouquet which he then waved about and sniffed. Zarren gathered a handful of lambs-ear leaves, softer than silk under his fingertips.

"If you keep waving those about, people will think you've gone mad."

Elijob sneezed. "Let them think so! I'd rather have fun than worry about what people think."

His twin's eyes lit up with an eager grin, his left hand slashing dramatically at tall stalks of grass like a sword. "Say, Zarren, maybe our life-long dream can come true now. We can train to become swordsmasters! Then travel the world and rescue every damsel and fellow in distress, just like real heroes."

Zarren laughed at Elijob's antics. "We have to find a swordsmaster who's willing to train us. Hopefully one who is extremely patient with odd poets."

"What are you trying to say? I'm a fast learner! I've got magnificent focus!"

"As magnificent as a puppy's."

"Do not!"

Afternoon came, and they sat in the tall, wildflower-littered grass for a quick meal, stuffing crispy bread and chunks of cheese into their mouths. They gazed up at patches of blue sky poking holes through the clouds.

Insects and honeybees drifted from flower to flower lazily. One brown butterfly with orange speckles batted its wings at a much larger butterfly: cream with yellow-green splashes and purple eye spots, battling for space. Even a rare sunburst swallowtail made an appearance, all the colors of a sunset along double sets of long tail-like wings. Barn swallows chirped as they swooped in graceful dives along the fields, open mouths catching up beetles and gnats.

"So, this is what adventure smells like." Elijob sniffed the air, breathing in deeply. "Like honey and sky and churned dirt."

Zarren choked on a piece of cheese. "Should I add that quote to our journal, chronicling the lives of the soon-to-be Bladeers, or the soon-to-be poet?"

Elijob elbowed him.

3

The clouds had turned lavender and slate-blue, and stripes of crimson slashed the horizon and setting sun, when at last they reached the city of Draethvyle, its grand spires rising above the city wall.

Instead of entering through the wide northern gate, the twins followed a second dirt path to enter through the eastern wall—where an almost-town, made of shabby wooden structures and open market stalls, crammed against Draethvyle's side. Zarren hoped there'd be fewer guards here—fewer people to remember the twins, in case *that man* came looking for them.

They strode along the winding street, past rickety houses, and laundry hanging out on lines above, vendor tents and tables full of cheaply made items. Homeless elders sat in shadowed corners, and grubby children ran past with a ball playing some game, weaving through the evening crowd.

Zarren spotted a young boy about his age, sprawled atop one of the many shop awnings. The blond boy with curious side-bangs met his gaze briefly, twiddling a grass stalk in his mouth.

'I wonder what sort of life he has here?' Zarren thought.

The dirt street ended at a gate and several guards. Zarren took out the leather fold and the money within, paying the steep entry fee, and answering questions in a simple way that wouldn't catch the guards' interest.

Just past the gate, the world became a sophisticated place of stone structures and mixed cobblestone and pavestone roads. "If we can reach the center of Draethvyle, we should be safe," he repeated.

"Right! The Draev Guardian place, just like Mother said." Elijob nodded, tipping his head back to eye the soaring factory buildings they passed. "Maybe they've got a swordsmaster, and we can be his pupils and have a new home here!"

It was a nice thought, but Zarren didn't want to get his hopes up too much.

The street shadows around them lengthened by the time they stopped for rest. Elijob wanted to ride the tram, but Zarren wasn't sure where it would lead, and he was afraid of getting lost. On foot it was easier to keep track of directions.

They rested in a tunnel-like alley, away from any prying eyes. They weren't in the inner reaches of the city yet, but close, the streets here more refined. They ate another meal of bread and cheese, and rubbed aching leg muscles and sore, Healing feet.

"These shoes have killed my feet with blisters." Elijob yawned, eyes watery. "And my eyelids aren't staying open."

Zarren knew the feeling. Maybe it would be okay to take a short nap. He just wouldn't let himself sleep deeply, to be safe. "You can shut your eyes for a bit," he told him.

Elijob did so. "Mm, I can't wait to become a swordsmaster, and be just like the Three Bladeers," he said sleepily. "But even if things don't work out, you know, I'm still glad we ran away."

They slumped against the tunnel wall, an arm each around the other for security. Elijob's head fell against his shoulder, and quiet minutes passed.

Zarren drifted awake. He sat up with a start, berating himself for dozing off. "We should go," he said, and glanced over at Elijob.

But his twin wasn't there.

"Elijob?" he called, scanning every which way. Not seeing him in the alley tunnel, Zarren got to his feet and ran out into the twilight.

He came to an open space with a round fountain, water bubbling from a stone horse. Few people were walking the streets, and none of them Elijob. The shadows spread silently in the ebbing light.

Where was he? He would never wander off like this! Not unless…he had a good reason to.

A chill lanced through his limbs. He had to find him!

Zarren called out, trotting past alleyways and hidden nooks. The number of people around dwindled, until he found himself alone on the vacant cold-stone streets.

"He has to be somewhere…" Zarren whispered. He hurried up a narrow strip of steps, as it climbed up-hill to another street. The steps stopped and the street leveled out.

"Where are you?" Zarren began, then halted. His back stiffened. Every hair across his skin raised.

A dead-end side street branched off from where he stood, and there was a body lying on its side with a pool of red blossoming.

Unable to breathe, he raced across the distance between them, screeching to a stop at Elijob's side. He got down and tried to sit Elijob up in his arms. But before he could, Elijob's eyelids fluttered open, blood down one side of his face. More blood coming from a stab wound in the chest.

"Go…" Elijob struggled to speak, staring up into his face intently. "Run. You must—"

Zarren had only enough time to stand before a large shadow appeared at his back.

A flash of metal sliced as Zarren turned.

"*Nngh!*" Zarren raised a hand to his throat. Wetness dripped past his fingers, down to his collarbone. A thought drifted through his mind that his neck had been sliced, before his body collapsed. Everything felt cold, the world tilting.

"Zarren!" He heard Elijob's strained voice scream.

"*Heh*, that should finish you," said an all-too familiar gruff voice, the figure standing tall at the side street's mouth, a long-bladed knife in hand. "Thought you could escape? That I wouldn't be able to find you? That you could go live happy little lives without me?" *That man* chuckled at his own dark humor. "You know, that wench of a mother of yours looked shocked, too. Did she really think she could leave me? If I can't have her, I make sure no one else can either. And the same goes for you." He sneered. "Your names were the last words she spoke."

The blade was black silver—a metal that slowed and even halted vempar Healing; and, depending on where it cut, a sure way to kill a vempar.

That man continued laughing, and he turned away from them, pulling out a small bottle of strong drink and downing it.

The world swayed like a boat at the storming docks around Zarren, images hazy, sounds fading. The last thing he felt was the pavestones against him, the last thing he saw was Elijob— crawling to reach his side.

Once Elijob reached his brother, eyes welling tears, he held him. Elijob opened his mouth.

At the near point of death, when all was beyond hope, the only way for a vempar to save a person was to use the Healing Kiss: Not an actual kiss, but close enough to breathe all of one's *essence* into the dying person. But this came with a price few were ever willing to pay.

Elijob gently brushed loose strands of raven hair from Zarren's sweat-drenched face, lowering his forehead to touch against his. His lips near Zarren's, he took a deep, painful breath and slowly exhaled, that breath *breathing* into Zarren a ghostly blue light. It left his mouth, entering his twin—filling Zarren with life as the strange light glowed within him, shimmering along the cut across Zarren's neck.

As the light faded, so too did the deep cut, now Healed.

Zarren gasped in the air, filling his lungs, suddenly wide awake. Confusion creased his forehead, until his gaze focused on Elijob. His brother smiled, red spilling down a corner of his mouth. Then it dawned on him what his brother had done.

"Elijob!" Zarren sat up, catching his twin as Elijob slumped over, pale face lolling in the crook of his arm. "N-no, why did you…?" He couldn't finish. "Is that why you left, to lure *him* away from me?"

"Live on brother." Elijob tried to swallow, his voice no more than a fading whisper. "Become what…we always dreamed of. You can…do it." His fair blue eyes half closed. "I know…you can."

"E-Eli…" Zarren's throat seized up, and shock numbed all feeling in his limbs. He could only caress his twin's bloodied cheek as he lay in his lap.

"Don't…be sad. I want you…to be the one who lives."

"N-no." Zarren's voice broke.

"Will you…do that for me?" Elijob insisted.

Zarren tried to think, but there was nothing he could do—
he couldn't give back the life breath given to him.

"Live…Zarren. Lord God will take care of you." He tried to
smile. "I love…you."

Zarren's vision blurred and he tightened his chest against the
pain ripping his heart apart. So much he wanted to say, but the
words that left his lips were a soft "I love you" back.

The lines of Elijob's face and smile softened as the life in his
eyes died out.

"Brother…"

Heavy footsteps were approaching Zarren from behind.
"Brought you back to life, did he? How stupid and sweet of
him." *That man's* wretched voice cackled. "Oh, don't cry now.
You'll be joining him soon."

Elijob's words resonated through Zarren: *"Will you do that for
me?"*

He gently rested his twin's body upon the pavestones.
Mother, Brother…all that had made up his world was now
gone.

"Live…Zarren."

The blade flashed.

Zarren rolled as the long knife slashed the air where he'd
been kneeling. He quickly pushed up on his exhausted feet and
sprinted around the man and out of the side street.

It wasn't long before his ears caught the heavy footsteps
echoing after him. Zarren wasn't sure where he was going in
the faded twilight, or how he would escape alive. All he could
think was to keep both legs running, ignoring the burning in his
calves and thighs.

Passing by the same horse fountain, he ducked under an
archway and entered a small plaza lined with buildings and
arcades. Before he could reach the nearest alley, a jolting pain
struck his right leg from behind.

"*Ahk!*" He collapsed, grabbing at the pain to find the long knife embedded in his leg—thrown by the wicked man who was now almost on top of him.

His teeth gritted against the pain as he grabbed the knife hilt and yanked it free. The black silver wound wasn't going to Heal anytime soon. He cast about. He needed a diversion, anything that would buy him time to run!

Diversion…diversion…

Kaw-kaw!

Zarren turned to see a single raven diving through the air.

Diversion…

As he watched, the raven split into *two* ravens. *Three* ravens. An entire *flock* of ravens. And all of them dove at *that man's* eyes.

"Shoo, you filthy—!" He cursed and waved his arms, trying to swat the black feathers away. Zarren kneeled there, dumbfounded for a moment, then moved, limping as fast as he could.

The ravens seemed to melt and swirl as fists struck them one by one, until they were all gone but the first original bird, who squawked and flapped upwards.

Zarren stumbled. He wasn't going to make it. He wasn't fast enough.

'*I tried, Elijob…*' he said in his mind. Clouds blanketed the sky, snuffing out the stars. '*I really tried.*'

"Now," the man began, breathing heavily from the effort, the veins in his eyes popping. He'd almost caught up to Zarren. "You're going to—" he started.

VHOOM!

A mass of wind in the shape of a diving falcon soared down, slamming the man flat on the pavestones—the force so hard that the stones webbed cracks.

Unable to move, the man stared blankly at the sky, lying face-up.

"You despicable soul."

Zarren tipped his face up to the clouds and saw a vempar gliding down through the air, landing black leather boots smoothly upon the ground. A gust ruffled his blue Draev cape and light brown hair, his eyes like twin rivers—Zarren recognized him: the one who'd been preaching in their hometown, only now in full Draev Guardian form.

The Draev bent an invisible fist of air to grab *that man*. "You are under arrest for murder and abuse," he said, voice quivering darkly. "I found the woman you killed. It was so obvious, as if she *wanted* to be found, to see you caught for your crimes and face justice."

Zarren trembled, realizing his mother had never intended to meet up with them, but rather to save them from the same fate.

An invisible gag sealed off the man's protests, and ropes of air tied and dragged him along as the Draev approached Zarren, his blue and silver cape swishing.

His gaze softened on the boy. "I am Draev Master Nephryte." He inclined his head. "Are you injured? We can take care of that. You're safe, now."

His hand reached out. Zarren stumbled backwards.

Nephryte frowned a fraction, then took back his hand and faced away. "You have Ability, it seems. I saw your illusions with the raven. I'll have to take you with me to Draevensett Academy. Don't worry, it's a nice place."

Zarren slowly began to follow him. But as soon as they left the plaza, he took off at a mad dash in the opposite direction, still limping.

"Wait! Young boy!" Nephryte trotted after him, up a flight of steps and to the left, into a dead-end side street.

Zarren got down and slid his arms underneath Elijob's cold body, lifting him up. It was too late for a Healing Kiss to save him now. A single raindrop fell, followed by more light drops pattering on the pavestones. His arms were sore to the point of breaking, but he would carry Elijob, no matter what.

Nephryte stood motionless, trying to smooth the look of horror from his features, as the raven-haired boy came back, the body of who must be his twin held in his skinny arms. The knife wound in his leg bled from beneath the pants fabric.

Nephryte cleared his throat. "Come. We'll find a peaceful place for your brother to rest," he told him quietly.

Raindrops fell like soft tears from the heavens as Master and small boy walked on through the night.

4

Z artanian's fingers flowed gracefully along the ivory keys of the organ, sunlight reflecting bright upon the silvery pipes.

He closed his eyes, not needing to watch his fingers as they hit every note, feeling it—recalling the first time he'd sat here and touched the keys, back when he was still new to Draevensett, more than three years ago…

Zarren's pale hand brushed aside grass and set a bouquet of wildflowers before the gravestone, inscribed with Elijob's name.

He sat there all morning long on his knees, silent tears dripping with the rain. Master Nephryte waited several paces back, solemn as he held an umbrella. A damp breeze tilted the rain and Zarren narrowed his gaze against it.

Elijob wanted him to live on, but how could he keep on living when the person who made it worthwhile was gone?

"Become what we always dreamed of… Lord God will take care of you."

"Is God really our hope, through the fiercest of storms?" he asked without looking back, recalling what Master Nephryte had preached that day in their hometown, which now felt so long ago.

"For those who cling to Him and follow His words, yes," Nephryte answered. "You have to get to know Him, first." Zarren turned his head at the feel of a hand on his shoulder. "Come. Your room in Draevensett should be ready."

Zarren shied away from the Master's hand, then looked embarrassed and apologetic. "Sorry…" he mumbled, not wanting to offend the only person who'd been kind to him.

Nephryte gave a reassuring smile, taking his hand back. "It's fine. Don't feel bad. You have the right not to let anybody touch you; it's your body." He straightened, holding the umbrella out for Zarren to walk under. Zarren strode alongside him, keeping a gap between them as they left Draethvyle's cemetery grounds.

Draevensett Academy rose like a mythical castle, grander than anything Zarren's humble fishing town could ever imagine. As they entered the decorative gate, a pixit barked at him.

Zarren was given his own dorm room, high on Floor Harlow, where two other boys and Master Nephryte lived. All he could think of was how much Elijob would have loved this. He placed the old *Three Bladeers* book from their backpack in the forefront of a shelf, fingertips brushing the cover.

Lykale and Mamoru were much older than him, and he had hidden behind the Master's tall frame, peeking his head around, when they were first introduced.

Mamoru put on a warm smile, despite the vicious scar on his

cheek. "It's very nice to meet you."

Zarren peeked at him warily, then answered as quiet as a mouse, "…It…it's nice to meet you, too."

Master Nephryte hid a chuckle, glancing over his shoulder at the mop of raven hair hiding behind him. "Mamoru and Lykale are the last people you should be afraid of. I'd even say Mamoru is compassionate to a fault."

Mamoru's gaze flicked up at Nephryte. "Says the one who keeps bringing in strays all the time."

"*Hmph*, and you should be grateful I do, *young* Mamoru." Nephryte emphasized the last with a smirk.

"What's your name, then?" Lykale bent down, peering around the Master to better see Zarren.

Zarren stepped back and fidgeted. "I'm…Zartanian," he said.

Zarren was a different person, a different life—he couldn't be that name anymore. But Zartanian was his made-up fan name inspired by the Three Bladeers. No, now it would become something more: his swordsmaster name.

Lykale snorted. "You're more unusual than I thought. Do those antlers hurt growing out of your skull?"

"Lykale," Mamoru reprimanded, jabbing an elbow.

"Just curious."

Lykale wasn't the only one to point out and ask about his antlers in the Academy. Even though he was mostly vempar, kids still pestered him about it.

Later that evening, Master Nephryte found him in the study room pulling out a book titled: *Bladeers of Old*. "Ohhh, so you're a secret fan? Now I understand where *Zartanian* comes from."

Zartanian gave a start, turning around with the book in hand.

"No, no, take it." Nephryte gestured. "You can even keep the book, if you like. And you're welcome to read any of these." He took a seat in an armchair and tilted his chin thoughtfully.

"Do you have a dream, Zartanian?" he asked. "A goal you would like to reach one day?"

A moment of silence passed while Zartanian fidgeted with the book. "I want to become a great swordsmaster, and save lives," he said quietly.

Nephryte regarded him. "I see… Wait here a moment."

He left the study, then returned with a long, flat box. "I was a fan once of the Three Bladeers. I even had *this* made." He opened the box and lifted out a Bladeer hat, plopping it on Zartanian's head—deep blue, with long fluffy plumes.

Zartanian tilted the too-big hat. It covered his antlers nicely.

"You'll grow into it soon." Nephryte chuckled. But what he lifted out next caught Zartanian by surprise: a long scabbard containing a glittering rapier.

Dark, silvery pommel and basket handguard, it was a beautiful piece of craftsmanship, and the dark metal of the blade was tinted a deep red. He didn't have to know much about blades to feel there was something different and powerful about this one.

"I found this in your old house, while a team of investigators was searching through it, hidden away in a box," said Nephryte. "It's blood silver, one of the twelve Legendary Weapons. I don't know why your parents had it, but it's best we keep this secret. You're too young and inexperienced to use this now, anyway, but once you've grown and learned enough, this will be yours. Every swordsmaster needs a grand sword, after all."

A rapier. Zartanian was speechless, and for the first time since losing his brother, his lips formed a smile, if only for an instant.

Zartanian explored Draevensett's many levels and tucked-away paths, and one morning he stumbled upon a miniature ballroom, off down a narrow, secluded corridor.

There he discovered a grand organ of soaring silver pipes and detailed inlaid patterns of ivory webs and ancient symbols.

His pale fingertips rested upon the ivory and ebony keys, running smoothly up and down, testing the notes which hummed through the ballroom.

"So, you think you can play, do you?"

His hands froze above the keys and he turned on the bench to face the owner of that brisk, precise voice.

A man moved down the staircase and onto the marble ballroom floor, his layered dark hair slicked back from his forehead and harsh facial features.

Zartanian stumbled to his feet, giving a half bow. "A-a pleasure to meet you, sir. I am Zartanian."

The man stopped before him. "So I've heard. You may address me as Sir Swornyte." He observed the organ's polished keys. "Enjoy playing, do you?" Zartanian paused before nodding timidly. "Hm, hm, well... If you show talent, and perseverance, I may teach you to play properly."

Zartanian's heart lifted at that.

Sir Swornyte faced him directly. "Your Master has expressed to me your desire to study the arts of the sword, and has requested that I train you in the ways of becoming a swordsmaster." His analytical stare narrowed in a way that felt intimidating. "Is that what you want, *Zartanian*? Are you willing to heed my every word, do every task that I put you to, and practice-practice-*practice*?"

Zartanian jumped in his shoes while the last word echoed around them. He nodded, striving to look determined, while inwardly his heart pounded with a mix of emotions.

"I will. R-really, I will, Sir Snornyte. I mean—" He flinched at his mistake, "—Sir Swornyte."

The man's brow twitched slightly, but his brisk voice stated, "Very good then, young pupil."

His hand, the skin gray as a storm, tossed a wooden sword at his chest. Zartanian clumsily caught it.

"Shall we begin?" He raised another practice sword, the tip pointing at his heart.

"Yes, Sir!"

THANK YOU

Thank you for reading! Parts of this novella turned out darker than what I usually write, but it was for a purpose, to reflect reality and to remind us of those who are suffering. But where there is suffering, there is also hope—a hope that is real and lasting, and that can only be found in Jesus. No matter what we face here in this world, God can hold our hand and guide us through. We just have to reach out and take His hand first. To learn more about Him, visit:

PeaceWithGod.net/where-is-god

You can get **the bonus stories to Strayborn:** *Storm & Choice* plus another one of my books free on my website, in the Reader Insider Vault, where I hope you'll also come along on this author journey with me and follow my bookish updates!

You'll be the first to learn about new releases, get bonus content, my curated clean book lists, updates and more:

Madness Solver in Wonderland
"It's a crazy ride trying to keep the peace between both
Wonderland and Earth, solving mysteries, but somebody's
got to do it—and unfortunately that somebody is me.
Welcome to my nonsense life!"

Draev Guardians Book #2
Now Available!
And the stakes are higher than ever…

THE ALTEREDVERSE

Books in the *Alteredverse* are standalone tales that take place in our world, at different points in time, and they often feature the humanoid Altered Ones (which includes vempars). Read Portal to Eartha for the origin story of the Altered!

They can be read in any order. Some books take place during our time, and some far into the future. To see the full Timeline of events, and where each book fits, visit the Reader Insider Vault's Bonus Material page:

eerawls.com/reader-insiders

Suggested reading order:

- *Frost, Winter's Lonely Guardian*
- *Portal to Eartha*
- *Beast of the Night*
- *Madness Solver in Wonderland*

Frost, *Winter Guardian and current resident of Boston.*
For centuries he's watched over the winter seasons, and
now he longs to end his work and move on from this
world. But for that, he needs a replacement, and the
human artist, Norah, might be the one—and the key
to thawing his icy heart.
A Jack Frost reimagining full of heart and wintery chill!

Future Japan.
A clue to a secret portal world.
The only hope for Lotus, an Altered girl with the gift of
Healing, on the run from the mafia…

You can get the ebook version FREE by joining
my newsletter at eerawls.com!

Beast of the Night

*A one-armed, practical girl. A rude lord hiding a curse.
A dark secret with the town's fate hanging in the balance…*

A Beauty and the Beast retelling with an
Austrian twist and a new breed of curse.

How You Can Help

Reviews help to boost a book on retailer websites so that it'll be found by more readers, which in turn helps support the author. *If you read the Draev Guardians book and want to share it with others, please consider leaving reviews on Amazon and Goodreads—* this makes a huge difference for indie authors like me! It doesn't have to be much, just click on how many stars you want to rate the book, and maybe add a sentence or two on your thoughts.

8 Ways to Support an Indie Author:

See a list of all the ways you can help support my work, as well as other indie authors!
Scan the QR code:

Ａᴜᴛʜᴏʀ

E.E. Rawls is the product of a traveling family, who even lived in Italy for 6 years. She loves exploring the unknown, whether it be in a forest, the ruins of a forgotten castle, or in the pages of a book. Her brain runs on coffee, cuddly cats, and the mysterious beauty of nature while she writes.

Visit her online at **eerawls.com** and get free access to the Reader Insider Vault:

Reader Insider Vault

Here You'll Get Access To:
- My Curated **No-Spice Book Lists**
- Bookish **News**, *Recs & Merch*
- **Behind the Scenes** details + First Looks + *Fun Bonuses* of my books
- **Free ebooks** & more!
- My **Exclusive Newsletter** & Substack: *where you can follow my author updates & fun random finds!*

eerawls.com
Scan QR Code